WHEN WE GET HOME

Focusing on novels with contemporary concerns, Bantam New Fiction introduces some of the most exciting voices at work today. Look for these titles wherever Bantam New Fiction is sold:

WHITE PALACE by Glenn Savan
SOMEWHERE OFF THE COAST OF MAINE by Ann Hood
COYOTE by Lynn Vannucci
VARIATIONS IN THE NIGHT by Emily Listfield
LIFE DURING WARTIME by Lucius Shepard
THE HALLOWEEN BALL by James Howard Kunstler
PARACHUTE by Richard Lees
THUNDER ISLAND by James Howard Kunstler
WAITING TO VANISH by Ann Hood
BLOCKBUSTER by Patricia A. Marx and Douglas G. McGrath
GOOD ROCKIN' TONIGHT by William Hauptman
SLIGHTLY LIKE STRANGERS by Emily Listfield
LOSS OF FLIGHT by Sara Vogan
WHEN WE GET HOME by Maud Carol Markson

BANTAM NEW FICTION

WHEN WE
GET HOME

MAUD CAROL
MARKSON

BANTAM BOOKS
NEW YORK · TORONTO · LONDON · SYDNEY · AUCKLAND

WHEN WE GET HOME
A Bantam Book / July 1989

Library of Congress Cataloging-in-Publication Data

Markson, Maud Carol.
  When we get home / Maud Carol Markson.
    p. cm. — (Bantam new fiction)
  ISBN 0-553-34660-1
  I. Title.
PS3563.A6717W4   1989
813'.54—dc19

Published simultaneously in the United States and Canada

Bantam Books are published by Bantam Books, a division of Bantam Doubleday
Dell Publishing Group, Inc. Its trademark, consisting of the words "Bantam
Books" and the portrayal of a rooster, is Registered in U.S. Patent and Trade-
mark Office and in other countries. Marca Registrada. Bantam Books, Inc., 666
Fifth Avenue, New York, New York 10103.

PRINTED IN THE UNITED STATES OF AMERICA

O   0 9 8 7 6 5 4 3 2 1

For Burton
and also for Alec Thunder

LOVE IS A FISH

In my family we are all disposable.

"People in your family are like geese," my boyfriend George once said in a rare moment of insight. "Always flying south and north."

"We fly to where the climate is right," I said, agreeing, and then, because I was feeling warm and tender toward George—it was the beginning of our times together—I said, "The climate is just perfect here."

George smiled, but it was not altogether sincere. For, of course, he was right. My parents had moved six times by my eighth birthday. There had been two career changes between them. My mother went back to school, my father sold one company, bought another. Each season they shipped off clothes and books, used furniture, linens, and even my toys to the Salvation Army.

"All through with *that*," my mother would say.

"Couldn't bear to see that old thing another week," my father might add.

It was no different with people. They favored and discarded friends as easily as others might frequent and later tire of a favorite restaurant.

"She's not quite as sharp as she used to be," my mother would say of a close friend.

"His tennis game has gone downhill," my father would add.

The following month there would be a new couple, attractive and full of promise, to take the old one's place. And then they too would be gone.

Nor were my brother and I spared. My mother often spoke of trading in Walter and me as if we were used cars. In fact, she eventually did trade us in. She left us with my father, had three children with her second husband, and has seen neither Walter nor I since. I sometimes imagined her new children, well-behaved and handsome, dressed in new clothes, and I wondered if they too would wear out.

My father was not much better. There were two wives immediately following my mother, and then the winter I turned twenty-one he was wed to another. I met him for lunch the week before the wedding and he gave it to me straight.

"Love is a guppy," my father told me that afternoon as we sat eating. We were in an elegant restaurant with lovely tulips on the table, fine china, and my father had ordered a good bottle of wine; it was to celebrate his new wife, he told me. Her name was Isabelle, and although I had met her a few times and even liked her, I couldn't see how she was so very different from the three who had gone before her.

2

"Love is a fish?" I said.

"A guppy," my father said. "It swims along famously. Reproducing at an alarming rate. But the guppy always gets swallowed up by something bigger." We were nearly done with lunch by this time and the bottle of wine was almost empty. Perhaps this talk meant nothing at all.

"Are you saying that love is insignificant?" I said, pushing my glass of wine aside. I had been living with George for a year and believed that, despite the troubles we sometimes suffered, George and I were destined for each other. I had told George I was in it for the long haul, and that when I loved a man he could count on it to last. Since then, George had already asked me twice to get married, and I sometimes thought that if he were to ask me again I would answer yes.

"Not insignificant, Annie," my father said, motioning the waiter for the check. "Particularly not to other guppies. I imagine they all look quite different to each other," he said. "Some even quite spectacular."

"But not to you," I said.

My father shrugged and gave me one of those looks I remembered so well from my childhood. If you were only a little wiser, the look said, just a bit sharper, you would understand.

"What about Isabelle?" I said. Isabelle was not as young as my father's third wife, nor as beautiful as my mother, his first, but she had a charming air about her. Walter and I, and even George, who vows he is charmed by no one, liked to watch Isabelle do things, the graceful way she walked around the house, the tilt of her head when she smiled, the way she touched her lips sometimes when she spoke, almost as if she were blowing a kiss. It would be easy to love a woman like Isabelle.

"Isabelle?" my father said. "An absolutely amazing

3

guppy.'' Then he grinned and stretched and looked particularly pleased with himself.

But I worried about my father, worried that it was not just love that got eaten up in his life.

At least there was always the summer house; we had not given that up yet. Despite my father's frequent notions to sell the house, and despite the efforts of two of his four wives to gain ownership of it during the battles over divorce, the house has remained with my family through two generations. It was one of only four houses on that side of the beach the year it was built, although now there were many more. Ours, like the other three from that earlier time, was white clapboard with red shutters and a large porch enclosing the house on three sides. When you walk down the porch steps in the back you are standing on soft white sand and staring out into the Atlantic Ocean. Walter and I loved the house. The floors were all dark wood and creaking, the windowsills were large enough to sit on. In the living room there were old photograph albums of my grandparents and my father when he was young. My grandmother made the quilts on the beds upstairs. There was even a watercolor my mother painted the year my parents were married—a picture of my father standing on the beach looking off toward the horizon. When my father threw it out after my mother left I retrieved it from the trash and hung it in my room near the window, and it was there still.

We have always spent our summers in the house and this year would be no different. My father would be there with Isabelle and she had brought her nine-year-old daughter Yvette. I was bringing George. And Walter, who had just broken off with another girl from school, was coming alone.

4

The others had already been in the house for over a month when George and I arrived. George could only take three weeks off from work and we had waited until August when the ocean was warmest and the heat in the city most unbearable before traveling to the beach. We took my old room on the third floor next to Yvette and looked forward to days of swimming in the ocean and quiet evenings getting slightly drunk before bed.

It was late at night when we arrived after a long drive out from the city, and everyone was already in bed. As George unpacked his clothing and folded it into the large chest of drawers, I opened the windows and smelled the familiar salt air. Then I showed George my mother's watercolor.

"She painted this the first year they were married," I told him. "It makes me cry to think of it."

"It's not very good," George said, looking up from his clothing. "See the strange definition between the sand and the sea. And your father—look what she did to his legs."

"You don't get it," I said, still staring at the watercolor. "She must have really loved him to paint him like that."

"Your father and mother have been divorced for over ten years," George said.

"That's not what I meant," I said. Of course, George was right about the painting; my mother was not an artist.

"Let's make love in the ocean while we're here," I said suddenly, changing the subject. "Let's do it some night."

"Oh sure," George said, and he grinned like a little boy. "You don't even like doing it if the sheets aren't clean."

5

"Well now I want to do it in the ocean," I said, and I kissed his neck and then his lips.

"You can count on it," George said. Then he got into bed and turned out the light. But I sat up for a while staring out the window at the ocean. The waves were lit up by the moon and I imagined myself swimming in the ocean with George, the current strong and powerful, the taste of the sea on our skin.

The next morning I slept late and George was already gone when I woke up. From the window I could see him and Walter out on the beach playing football. George, who is tall and muscular from years of high school and college sports, was a far better athlete than my brother. He threw the ball farther, missed fewer passes. Walter, however, was more fun to watch. He jumped up and down, yelled strange signals, and at one point took a quick run into the ocean clutching the football under his arm.

As I left the house to join them I passed Yvette sitting on the floor of her room alone, listening to a Sony Walkman. She was a thin girl with yellow hair and pale skin, dressed in long pants and a Berkeley sweatshirt.

"Hi Yvette," I said, but she didn't hear me. I entered the room, knelt down, and tapped her shoulder. "Hi," I said again.

She frowned, but turned the volume down on the tape. We had met only twice before: once at the wedding where she had unwittingly drank too much champagne and had thrown up all over her dress, and a second time at my father's for dinner.

"I'm going out to the beach," I said to her. "Do you want to join me?"

"I hate the ocean," she said and twisted a strand of her hair round and round her finger.

"You don't have to swim," I told her. "We can play football or fly my kite."

"There are green flies on the beach," she said.

"Come on," I tried one last time.

"I'm listening to music, if you can't see," she said. Then she turned the volume back up on the Walkman, pressed the back of her head against the bed, and looked away.

George and Walter and I played and swam out at the beach all morning. Then, at noon, Isabelle and my father joined us. Isabelle brought along a large picnic lunch, which she set out on a striped beach blanket. There were a cold lemon soup, cucumber and tomato salad, cheese sandwiches, and homemade almond cookies. My father carried one thermos containing lemonade and another with iced gin and tonics.

"Quite a lunch," George said, seating himself on the edge of the blanket.

"And quite the service," Walter said. He and Isabelle grinned at one another.

I hugged my father hello and kissed Isabelle politely on the cheek.

"You look lovely," she said to me. "And so thin."

"You're not starving her, are you?" my father said to George, and George blushed.

"Of course he's not," Isabelle said. "She looks wonderful."

"Oh, Annie always looks wonderful," Walter said.

I was not as beautiful as they were always telling me, but I did know that with my summer tan, new blue swimsuit, and my long hair bleached from the sun, I was

7

as pretty as I had ever been. Men watched me pass on the beach, the lifeguards waved hello.

"Enough," I said. I took the tall cold glass my father handed me and drank it quickly.

It was a pleasant lunch. Walter built a lopsided castle on top of Isabelle's bare feet. George talked to my father about an investment he was considering. And I kept the plates and glasses filled. When we were almost through eating—George and my father had already risen to resume the game of football—Yvette finally joined us down at the blanket. She was still dressed in long pants and, although she was not listening to any music, she carried the Walkman at her waist.

"Are you hungry, dear?" Isabelle said, looking up at her daughter. It was then, out there in the sun, that I noticed for the first time the similarity between them. The yellow hair, the long thin face, the angular body. Perhaps Yvette might still grow out of her present unloveliness and acquire all the grace and good looks of her mother.

"Aren't you hot?" Walter said to Yvette. "Where's that string bikini we all know and love so well?"

"I don't own a bikini, for your information," Yvette said.

I passed her a glass of lemonade and a sandwich and she went and sat on the far edge of the blanket, staring down at her lap.

My father waved at her between a pass. "Hey Yvette," he shouted, but she did not wave back.

"You could really use some sun," Isabelle said to her daughter. "Why not go up to the house and change into your suit?" Yvette did not answer.

Isabelle, who was wearing a pretty black swimsuit, slightly shook her head at her daughter. Then she lay down across the blanket and closed her eyes. Walter

8

poured out a puddle of suntan lotion and began to slowly massage the lotion over Isabelle's shoulders, down her arms, across the small of her back.

"I'm not interested in getting a tan," Yvette said to her mother. "There are other things in life, you know."

"Lighten up," Walter said, still working on Isabelle's back with the lotion.

Yvette looked like she might cry.

"I'm going to play football," I said finally. "Don't you want to join the men and get a real game going?"

"Okay," Yvette said. But she only played with us for a few minutes before going back up the beach to the house, the music from her Walkman blaring directly into her ears.

In the evening, Walter joined George and me at a neighborhood bar called the Seascape. It was built on a boardwalk that extended out to the ocean and was crowded with suntanned people, talkative and energetic after a day on the beach. There was a jukebox playing the songs that were popular that summer, and after two drinks Walter coaxed me onto the dance floor.

He sang in my ear as we danced.

"You're silly," I said to him.

"Of course I'm silly," he said. "It's a curse." Then he twirled me under his arms and we both started giggling. George, still sitting at the table, ordered another round of beers from the waitress, and when I caught his eye I smiled. I was enjoying the music and the energy I felt from dancing. I liked it that George was watching me; I felt pretty and happy, and when I looked at him again he smiled back.

"Baby we were born to run," Walter was singing as we danced, and he did a small leap in the air. "I've been practicing," he said. Then, looking serious for a moment, he said, "How do you think Dad's doing?"

"He seems happy enough," I said. "For now, anyway." I was thinking of his talk at the restaurant about love and fish.

"How could he not be happy with a woman like Isabelle?" said Walter.

"She is nice," I said. Then a young man in a Hawaiian shirt and shorts cut in on our dancing, pulling me away, and Walter went back to join George and the beer.

"Is that your boyfriend?" the man asked me as we danced.

"No." I shook my head.

"Your husband?" he said.

"He's my brother," I said.

"Well, then hell, let's dance," he said. He pulled me close and I danced with him and then with three of his friends for quite a long time.

That night when we returned from the bar George and I had a big fight.

"You ignored me all night," George said. "You acted as if you didn't want to be with me."

"I was dancing," I said.

"Not with me," George said. He pulled off his shirt and threw it on the floor. "You danced with everyone but me."

"Oh really," I said. Of course it was true, but I had not meant it to be that way. I wanted to please George, make him happy, but I had wanted to please the men at the bar as well. "They asked me to dance," I tried to explain. "I couldn't say no."

"We're supposed to be a couple," he said. Then he lay back across the bed as if he had resigned himself to the fact that perhaps we weren't.

"We are a couple," I said.

"You're different when you're around your family," George said, and his voice sounded as if it were coming from far away. "Like them."

I wasn't like my family, but I didn't say anything. Instead I picked up his shirt and hung it neatly in the closet. Then I knelt down and pulled off his shoes; something about his sadness made me suddenly want him very badly.

"You become like *them*," said George as I pulled off his socks and kissed his ankles.

"Anne," he said. "Are you listening? I said you become just like them."

Then I unbuttoned his fly. George sat up quickly, very nearly pushing me over. "Don't touch me," he said. "I'm not in the mood."

"What do you mean?" I said.

"You know what I mean," he said, and he buttoned up his pants.

"Fine," I said. "Just fine." But I was already in tears by the time I had left the room.

I walked down the hall past Yvette's room, where the door was closed tight. Then down the creaking old staircase. The house was very quiet and dark, but when I got to the living room there was a light on and Walter was lying on the couch reading. Walter was thin and tall like me, but fairer, with freckles, like our mother. I knew that women found him attractive, always had, his sincere face, his youthfulness. But tonight, in his terry cloth robe and white sweat socks, I saw only my little brother, pouting, deep in thought.

"Annie," he said when he saw me. "Primo dancing." Then he noticed my tears. "Hey, what's wrong?" he asked. "You and your true love have a fight?"

11

I shrugged, and he moved over on the couch to make room for me to sit down.

"Don't worry about George," Walter said. "Good men like him are easy to find."

"Don't you dare make fun of him," I said, and I started to cry all over again. "Don't you like him?"

"Of course I like him," Walter said. He put his book down on the floor and handed me the end of his robe to wipe my eyes. "There's nothing not to like about George."

"Well, you talk about him as if you were making fun of him," I said.

"I'm sorry," Walter said, and he sounded sincere. "I just don't think he is going to be your last and only love."

"What do you know about real love, anyway?" I said. "George and I are perfect for each other."

Walter took a deep breath; his chest rose and then fell. Then he told me. "I'm in love with Isabelle," he said.

"What do you mean?" I said, knowing of course what he meant.

"We're sleeping together," Walter said.

"I don't believe you," I said.

"And I'm madly, incredibly in love with her," Walter continued.

"You are really sick," I said. I moved away from him on the couch, not wanting to be near him any longer.

"I know you don't believe me, Annie, but I've never been so in love before. I couldn't stay away from her if I tried."

"You sound really stupid," I said.

Walter shrugged. "This is *it*," he said. "Or as near as *it* gets."

"You're sleeping with her," I said, and I found myself whispering without even trying.

"For a month now," Walter said. "On the days when Dad goes into the city to work."

"Doesn't she know she's married to Dad?" I said. I felt a sickness in my stomach and then in my throat. I picked up one of the pillows from the back of the couch and pressed it against my chest. I wasn't even sure why it bothered me so much. My father had never been possessive about his women—they came, then went. And although Isabelle was in her mid-thirties, Walter was only twenty; he didn't know what marriage was all about. Perhaps none of us did. "She's married to Dad," I repeated.

"I want her," Walter said.

"She's already taken," I said.

"But I want her now," Walter said. He sounded as he had as a child, whining about something in the store he wanted my father to buy.

"Does Dad know?" I asked.

"No," he admitted. "But I think Yvette does. You know how kids are."

"Yvette?" I said.

Then I really began to cry. I wouldn't let Walter touch me and I couldn't stop crying. I pushed the pillow against my face and then threw it at Walter.

"You're going to get hurt," I said. "She's not going to even think about you when we leave the house at the end of the summer."

"Don't be like that, Annie," said Walter. "It doesn't become you."

"I don't care," I said. Then I ran out of the room and out of the house, across the porch, and into the darkness of the beach.

George and I made up in the morning.

"I'm sorry for making you leave last night," George

13

said to me on his way to the bathroom. There was a slight crease on the side of his face from where he had slept on it during the night. His eyes looked not yet awake. "I was really dumb," he said.

"I was, for not dancing with you," I said.

Then George put his arms around me and I smelled his morning breath and didn't mind. "I was really dumb for not making love to you," he said.

I kissed him and we both smiled.

"And I was really dumb for hurting you," he continued.

"It's okay," I said. And it was.

Out on the beach that afternoon George and I were playful. We dove over each other in the water and ran down the beach together to where a large jetty had been built out across the sand. At one point, while we were sitting together on the wall, holding each other tight, I thought of telling George about Isabelle and Walter. But I didn't know how to begin, and I did not want to hear George's voice as he calmly predicted my family's demise.

For the rest of the summer I avoided Walter. I thought it would be difficult but I was wrong. On weekends when the whole family was together I swam long distances in the ocean, and when I came out I only spoke to my father and to Isabelle and George. During the week, when my father drove into the city to work, Walter and Isabelle disappeared together. They were not so foolish as to do it in the house where Yvette might find them—or worse, George or I would—but I knew they were together somewhere, in a hotel room in town or perhaps somewhere down the beach where it was quiet and not yet built up.

George and I never did make love in the ocean that summer, but it was a relaxing vacation and we were happy. We even got Yvette to smile one day, out near the water flying my kite. George let her hold the string for a while and promised to buy her her own kite which he did the very next day, and her face lit up at his kindness.

The first week in September we all left the house. George and I were expected back at work. And the day before, Yvette had been put on a train for Connecticut, where she went to school. Walter too was going back to school. Isabelle and my father were to drop him off at the airport, where he would catch a late-night flight to Chicago. We all seemed rather anxious to depart, to get back to doing what we had left. Isabelle surveyed the house to make sure nothing was left behind, and my father called the cleaning service to have them come in the next day and close the house down for the winter.

"We really should sell this old house," my father said as he hung up the phone. "It's getting harder and harder to keep it up. And the neighborhood's not as nice as it used to be."

"What's wrong with the neighborhood?" I said.

"I think I know what your father means," George said. Then, seeing my look, he quickly picked up our bags and headed out with them to our small rental car.

"We thought we might buy a share in a ski house this winter instead," Isabelle said.

"You can do both," I said.

"There are a lot of sad memories in this house," my father said, and, swinging one of Isabelle's cases over his shoulder, he too began walking toward the cars.

"There are also a lot of great memories in this house," said Walter. He grinned at Isabelle, but she did not look back. Instead, she shrugged her shoulders and joined my father outdoors.

"Don't worry," I said to Walter as we huddled over the remaining belongings. "He won't sell the house. He's been talking like this for years."

"I don't know," Walter said, holding his duffel bag in one hand, my kite in the other. "Maybe this time he really will." Although he was talking to me, he was staring out through the screen door at Isabelle. He had a strange sad expression that had nothing to do with my father or the house. And I knew suddenly that I had been right from the start; it was over between him and Isabelle. She was going back to the city with my father, whom I believed she did love in some way. And Walter was going back to the Midwest to finish up his senior year. I was relieved it was over, that my father's new marriage could continue as it should, and I was certain that when we next all met, Walter would be with someone new—a young freshman from school, pretty and unattached.

Out by the cars we all hugged and kissed and promised that we would see each other soon.

"Don't be a stranger, Annie," my father said. "I miss you too much, and Isabelle loves to have someone like you around."

George thanked my father and Isabelle for making him welcome at the house.

"We hope you're going to be a permanent member soon," my father said to George and shook his hand.

"I'm counting on it," said George.

Walter held my hand and walked me out to the car, picked with his finger at the rental car sticker in the window.

"Call me," I whispered in his ear. Now that it was over between him and Isabelle I felt sad that I had avoided him these three weeks of our summer together; I would probably not see him again for a long time.

"I'll call collect," said Walter.

I rolled my eyes and Walter kissed me loud on the lips. "Bye, bye, Annie," he said. Then we were all gone.

*   *   *

I did not talk to Walter again until the week before Christmas. George and I had been invited to my father's for Christmas day and I was sure that Walter, who would be on vacation from school, had been invited as well.

It was a gray rainy day when I called Walter, and it had been like that for weeks. George and I had also been fighting a great deal, loud horrible fights. We had even fought that morning over something I couldn't remember. George, without even an umbrella, had gone out in the rain to his office where he could be alone.

"I don't know what's wrong with us, Anne," he said as he left the house.

I wasn't sure what was wrong between us either, except that George wanted very badly to get married, and I had spent two afternoons making love to a man I had met at the gym and thought about it sometimes when I was alone with George at night. I am sure that sounds terrible, but I did not do it to hurt George, nor to punish him for our arguments, our shortcomings. I did it because the man at the gym seemed to want, or even expect it. He was slightly balding with wet triangles of perspiration on his chest and under his arms. And when he talked to me that first time, it was with false confidence, like Walter's, and hope that yes I would meet him for a drink and then just maybe later we would go to bed. He seemed so grateful to talk, I could not turn him down nor leave him standing there sadly, alone.

It had been that way too the first time I met George, only much more so.

I was a senior at college, and it was at a party given by a friend. That night she promised she would introduce me to an older man, a law student at the school, and I had rolled my eyes.

17

"That ought to be real exciting," I said.

But when I finally met George I was impressed by how much older he did seem, so much more sure of who he was, what he wanted. My own experiences seemed small indeed.

"I'm going to be a defense attorney," he told me as we stood together in a tight corner, far away from the sweet smell of marijuana coming from the joints and pipes being passed around. George told me he liked his head to be always clear, and then he spoke with such fervor about his studies that he seemed to exclude all others in the room, including me. It was both compelling and disturbing.

"I want to be the kind of lawyer that really helps people," he added finally. Then, after an apologetic pause, as if he realized how corny he might sound, he looked at me closely. "What do you want to do, Anne?" he said.

The Stones were playing on the stereo and I wanted to dance. I wanted to forget about college midterms and my family back in New York. I wanted a tall cold drink. But that wasn't what George meant. Even I knew that. So even though I had not yet thought of doing it, had never done it on a first or even a fourth date, I told him I wanted to make love to him.

"That's what I want to do," I said to George.

He lost his composure for the first time that evening. His laugh was high-pitched, he leaned back against the wall.

"I just meant what you wanted to do when you grow up," he said.

"Oh," I said. "I knew that."

Then he smiled, and gently touched my hair. He seemed so earnest, so stable, and he was handsome as well. Taller, even than me, with white-blond hair, and when he looked at me his eyes were very blue.

"Really? You want to?" he said, and then, "We don't have to."

But of course we did make love that night. I had not wanted to disappoint him. In my life, men always seemed to have such expectations, and now, as I dialed Walter's number in Chicago, I worried about the day all my small efforts would fail.

When Walter finally answered my call he pretended not to know it was me.

"Annie who?" he said.

"Don't be silly," I said, but I was happy to hear his voice.

"Oh, it's you," he said. "Mrs. George."

"I'm not married to George," I said.

"Well Merry Christmas, anyway," he said.

We talked for a while. He told me about a writing course he was taking at school, about his apartment on the South Side of Chicago, and about the part-time job he had found. "I sell mobile car phones," he said. "Sometimes to people who don't even own cars." He laughed too loudly.

I asked him if he was seeing anyone, and when he said no, I asked him if he was coming to our father's for Christmas.

There was a long silence on the phone. Then, "I still love her," he said. "I miss Isabelle."

"No you don't," I said and felt a tightness in my throat. Strangely, I was hopeful that he did still love Isabelle, that I was wrong, that love could last. "No you don't," I said again.

"Yes I do," said George. "I really do."

Then he told me he was spending the holidays with a friend in Colorado and that he had sent me and George a pornographic videotape for Christmas.

"We don't need things like that," I said.

"Then send it back," Walter said. "Because I sure do." With that he hung up the phone.

I sat alone in the kitchen holding the receiver in my hand and I missed Walter very badly. Then I missed George too, although I had seen him only that morning. I was angry at myself for fighting with him, and angrier, and sorry too, that I had spent those afternoons with the man from the gym. I didn't even like the man all that much. Suddenly, I knew for the first time since George and I had been together that I truly wanted to get married. I wanted a big wedding with a white dress and brides-maids and lots of rice and my father to cry and give me away. I wanted to live forever with George. I imagined us together, older, in a house somewhere, talking about the neighbors or the children we would have. It was all perhaps a romantic notion of getting married, but for now it was real and I wanted it. Then I called George at his office with the happy news.

IN TRANSIT

Our wedding was riddled with the tension that divorced families seem to bring to holidays and important occasions. I vividly remembered crying the morning of the ceremony because my mother, whom I had invited under duress, had refused to wear the same type of flowers in her corsage as Isabelle.

"I am mortified that you would even consider it," my mother said to me.

Later in the day a childhood friend of George's put his arm around me and breathed heavily onto my neck.

"How well do you know George?" he said to me.

"Well enough," I said.

"Not like I know George," he said. Then he added, "Watch out. He's not just your average guy. Not if you really know him." And menacingly, if not quite painfully, he nipped my ear.

If that had not been enough, Walter drank far too much and my father flirted all evening with an old school friend of mine.

I had not spoken to any of them since, and when Walter called me from school I thought it was to apologize for his behavior at the wedding, to apologize for everyone's behavior. And in Walter's own way I suppose it was.

"Our family is a forgiving bunch," Walter started out.

"I hardly think so," I said.

He was calling me collect and I could hear what sounded like his roommate in the background; he was throwing a ball against the wall over and over again. Thump-pause, thump-pause, thump-pause. "Walter," I asked him, "what have you done wrong?"

He laughed that low contagious laugh of his. "Nothing yet," he said, and I laughed with him, feeling familiar and young again.

In the background I could still hear the thumping of the ball, almost like a metronome it was so steady. "There's this girl," I heard Walter saying over the phone.

"A girl," I said.

"I slept with her friend," Walter said. "Actually her roommate. And now she won't speak to me. When I call she hangs up the phone." The thumping in the background had finally stopped; the ball had fallen or the roommate had tired and quit. "You wouldn't act that way, would you, Annie?" Walter said. "If you were my girl?"

"I'd kick you in the balls," I said.

"Did you hear that?" Walter was saying to his roommate. "My own sister would kick me in the balls."

I could hear the roommate laughing somewhere in the background, a loud snorting kind of laugh, and then Walter was laughing too.

"Is this what you called to tell me?" I said.

"But you would speak to me, wouldn't you?" Walter continued. That brought on another giggling snort from his roommate, as if Walter was making faces at him from across the room. "You have a very forgiving nature," he said.

"Not now, I don't," I said loudly to both of them, but I was smiling. "And next time call me on your own dime."

"Oh Annie," Walter said, but I hung up the phone.

Later, however, I thought about it, about us being forgiving. Perhaps we were a family that had more to forgive than other families. I was thinking of my father's repeated attempts and subsequent failures at marriage. And I thought of my mother. When we were young and still all together, my mother once took me aside while we were shopping for new school clothes and told me that if it were not for me and Walter her life would have been far richer, far more complete. We were in the dressing room and I still remember I was trying on a green plaid jumper, which seemed to me old-fashioned, childish. The tag in the back scratched the nape of my neck. Yet it turned out that jumper was the only item of clothing we bought that day, and later when I wore it I felt it protected me from some adult life I did not want to enter. Although this was during a time when Walter and I shared everything, I did not repeat to him my mother's words. It was not so much that I was fearful of hurting Walter; I just did not want him to hate her.

Walter and I were not perfect children either. At sixteen I once ran off with my boyfriend, ending up in

Burlington, Vermont, for the weekend (although I called
my father as soon as we arrived), and Walter was reputed
to be a terror at school. George, who had heard my stories,
has often told me that Walter and I would never have
survived in his family.

"In my family," George told me, "there were rules
and we obeyed those rules."

"But were you happy?" I asked him, and I thought of
George's solemn parents. They spoke little when I came
to visit and moved cautiously around each other, and
particularly around George as if just by moving too quickly
or breathing too hard they might cause irreparable damage
—take his eyes out, or paralyze him from the waist down.

"Of course I was happy," George said to me. But I
have found that George does not like to question much in
life. I once found him reading a book on death called *The
Final Element*. He was as embarrassed as if I had caught
him leering at a *Penthouse* centerfold.

The apartment where George and I lived was too
small. It was really just one large room. A counter separated the kitchen from the living room area, and an alcove
held our bed and chest of drawers. If you were in the
kitchen you could see who was lying on the bed. Our
books were piled high atop the windowsill. You could
watch television from anywhere in the apartment. We had
thought sometimes of moving; we could afford something
larger now, but I had grown accustomed to the neighborhood. I knew where to buy the best produce and the
freshest fish. The old man in the bakery gave me free cups
of coffee and admired my legs and my long blond hair.
And I could walk to the bookstore where I work. George,
who had to take the subway to work downtown, did not
want to move either. He found something honorable about

living in our small space, as if we were thereby providing larger apartments for the rest of the world.

"In other parts of the world, entire families live in rooms smaller than this," George told me.

"But they have no choice," I said.

George was also concerned about money. He worked for a large corporate law firm and was often saddened by the problems that beset the clients he represented.

"They're all money problems," George had often said. "The problems big money creates."

"Someone has to help the fortunate," I had assured him, but he was unconvinced.

"These people don't know what real unhappiness is like," George sometimes said. "They have only known an untroubled life."

I disagreed with him. I believe we are all plagued with a life that is just beyond our control, that even those of us who appear to be the most fortunate, the most untouched by sadness—who live in large houses with polished wood floors, who fly off to islands in the winter and ski in the spring, who have beautiful children and loving husbands or wives—must worry about the day it will all disappear.

George had told me this was naive, that hunger was hunger and death was death, and that could not be confused with what we imagined. I shrugged.

For the most part, however, George and I had gotten on well since we married. There were worse wives; I was not slovenly or mean. I enjoyed making love to him, and we did it often. I thought about George when I was shopping and I bought him foods he liked. And George was a good husband. He was helpful around the apartment, remembered special occasions with expensive and thoughtful gifts, and he encouraged me.

25

"Look for a new job," he sometimes suggested. "Join a book club. Go skydiving if you like." There was little George considered beyond my ability.

I suppose the only bad thing that could be said about our marriage was that despite our small apartment, we seemed to remain in two different worlds. We did not share our drinks or food, or even the same space on our bed; each of us lay on our backs, arms close at our sides. I imagined us often as two drawings in a coloring book. We were on the same page, but there was a black outline around our bodies. We did not go out of the lines, and though I found it at times unbearably lonely, I did nothing. At least I did not until the accident.

I heard about it for weeks, perhaps even months afterward, until I almost believed I had been with George when it happened, or sometimes even that I had been there instead of George. It was that real.

It happened on George's way home from work. He was on the subway moving uptown from Wall Street. There was no free seat, and he stood with his briefcase tucked between his knees and a newspaper under his arm, an unsteady position on any ground. There was a Korean woman sitting in the seat in front of him, but she did not look toward him or the other passengers, but instead twisted her neck so that she was looking out the window. George could see her face reflected in the glass, slightly askew, as if the dirt from the window were actual blemishes on her skin. Above the woman's head someone had scrawled DEATH TO ALL BANANAS in yellow paint. There was an older man standing next to George; their shoulders were touching. George had seen the man before on the train. Like George, he carried a briefcase and wore a suit; he had a kind face and carried lollipops in his breast pocket. George imagined the man had grandchildren somewhere nearby, that he would give them the lollipops that night when he arrived home. Perhaps none of this would have been remembered if it weren't for the accident.

They were pulling out of the second station when the train suddenly jolted to an abrupt stop. The lights flickered on and off twice, and then off for good. The old man lost hold of his briefcase and the lollipops bounced out of his pocket, red, yellow, and green. A woman screamed. The car rocked and George fell face forward into the Korean woman's lap. This was not the ordinary jolting of the subway; word traveled through the car fast: A young girl had thrown herself under the train.

"She was white," a black man said.

"She was carrying a red knapsack," said another man who claimed to have witnessed her jump.

"Are you sure someone didn't push her?" someone else asked.

And a woman who had fallen to the floor when the train stopped just sat there. "She was so young," the woman said.

The Korean woman looked at George aghast. He could smell her unusual perfume, could feel her thin legs beneath her dress. He almost didn't want to move his face, but, blushing, he straightened himself up, picked up his own briefcase and then that of the old man's. He also picked up the man's lollipops from underneath the seat where they had fallen, and he handed them to him.

"Give those to me," the old man said and grabbed them so quickly out of George's hand that they fell again to the floor. The man left them there, took his briefcase, and pushed through the crowd of people and into another car.

The Korean woman neatened her skirt and closed her eyes for a moment as if she were saying a brief prayer.

27

"I'm so sorry," George said, but she said nothing in reply.

The subway car still didn't move and people began to grumble about the heat and the darkness. Two teenage boys started shouting, "Move, move, move, move," and others took up the chant as well. A baby started crying. George held on to the hand grip so tightly that his knuckles hurt and he thought of the young girl under the tracks. Although he had not actually seen the accident, George imagined the subway workmen picking up the remains of the body out from under the train. George saw her young face, desperate and scared, as she leaped from the yellow line painted on the edge of the platform. He saw her small black shoes fall in flight. The other people on the train had already stopped talking about the young girl; they merely wanted to get off the subway out into the fresh air, where they could forget what had happened. And eventually the subway did move, the lights flickered back on, and George arrived safely at home.

We read about the accident in the evening paper and listened to it on the news.

"I can't imagine why she would do such a thing," George said. We were lying in bed watching pictures of the girl flash for the third time across our television screen. Her name was Maria Bender and she was seventeen years old. She had two small brothers and her parents owned a grocery store near the Village. They all appeared together— her parents, her two brothers—in our small apartment, solemn and near tears.

"She had so much to live for," George said.

"I suppose just not enough," I said. I turned off the television and tried to hold George in my arms, but he would not be comforted. He lay alone on his side of the bed, not touching me, not talking to me, and I imagined he was remembering his face falling into the Korean woman's lap, as if that were an approximation of the girl's fall, as unexpected, as sad.

The next morning George was still talking about the accident. He kept remembering more details.

"Did I tell you the old man dropped his lollipops?" he asked.

I nodded.

"Did I tell you the girl had long thick hair like yours?" he continued. "Did I tell you she was studying French? That she was on her way to class when she killed herself?"

Of course he had. The girl's tragedy was not ours, but it might as well have been. George acted as if he had lost his sister or daughter. He even contacted her parents late one evening.

He reached Mrs. Bender; I could tell from the soft way George spoke that it was the girl's mother.

"I just called to tell you I was there," I heard George say over the phone. "On the subway that killed her. I'm very sorry."

I do not know what her mother said in reply; I am sure she was stunned and somewhat confused. I am sure the phone call frightened her—a strange man late at night talking about her daughter as if he had known her or even pushed her off the platform himself. It certainly frightened me.

I cannot say this one girl's death changed our marriage. Rather, it seemed to exaggerate what was already there. In the past, George had insisted we lead our separate lives. He had his job, I had mine. In the evenings and on weekends we were apart. I would go to a museum or, if it was warm, to the park. At night I swam laps at the gym near our home. George did not go with me. Instead, he joined a photography class. He once even took a course on how to better your chances at casino gambling, although George had never gambled in his life.

"I'm only trying to improve myself," he had told me, as if it were all part of some larger plan.

I sometimes suggested that we spend more time together, share an activity that we both enjoyed—isn't that what married people did? George looked always as if he had been slapped.

After the accident our lives became more distant, more remote. We made love infrequently and when we met at dinner we barely spoke, but stared at each other blankly like two fish in a bowl. I continued my own activities in the evening but George quit all his clubs and classes. He began spending his time alone in the apartment at night; he watched television for hours on end, and sometimes when I came home I found him lying on the bed staring up at the ceiling, the TV a buzz in the background. I thought George was falling in love with the girl.

"Her tragedy is so real," he explained to me one evening as we finished dinner. "I've never known anything like it."

"Teenage girls commit suicide all the time," I said rather flippantly, and I got up from the table to do the dishes.

"You weren't there," said George. "You don't understand what it was like."

I turned the water in the sink on loud, but I could still hear him. "You've never known the pain that girl suffered," George went on.

"She killed herself," I shouted above the sound of the faucet. "What's so great about that?"

Startled, George looked at me for a moment. Then he shook his head, left the table, and got into bed. He did not take off his shoes and they made two lumps at the foot of the bed. At the top I could see his head peeking out from above the sheets like a burrowing creature sniffing the air for safety.

"Get out," George ordered me from the bed. "I don't want you here with me."

"Okay, I will go out," I said, but I didn't. I think I was scared to leave George and the apartment just then. I thought if I left I wouldn't be able to come back.

I cleaned the apartment instead. First I washed the dishes more thoroughly than usual, then instead of putting them on the rack to dry I did them each by hand and put them all away in the cabinet above the sink. I vacuumed and dusted, pulling down the stacks of books to wipe the windowsill clean. I put out the garbage and did a load of wash. In the bathroom I got down on my knees and scrubbed the tub and toilet and did not even flinch when I came across two roaches crawling in the corner near a crack. I squished them in a piece of Kleenex and flushed them away. George watched me clean from the bed and during some point in the evening he fell asleep. When I got into bed, exhausted, he did not move beside me.

The next morning, while I was looking for some lunch money in George's wallet, I came across a newspaper photograph of Maria Bender. She was not a particularly pretty girl, I noticed for the first time. Her nose was pudgy and her eyes were too close together. It was difficult to tell in the newsprint but it looked as if her face was scarred with acne. She did, however, have lovely long brown hair. It fell on either side of her face, smooth and thick.

31

YOUNG GIRL JUMPS UNDER SUBWAY TRAIN, the caption read. George was still asleep and I thought of tearing the picture up and throwing it away. Instead I folded the photograph and placed it back in the wallet. I took no money for lunch and did not kiss George good-bye.

At work I went into the back where the books were stored and priced. There was a nice odor of fresh paper and dust and it was cool and dark. Mrs. Nash, the owner, was there using the telephone in her small office, and when she hung up I asked her if I might make a call.

"Is it long distance?" she asked.

"I'll pay for it," I said, and she shrugged and handed me the phone. It was an hour earlier in Chicago and I prayed that Walter was still in his room.

His roommate answered the phone in his loud voice, and when he told me Walter was sleeping I ordered him to be woken.

"What do you want?" Walter said, his voice foggy with sleep.

"It's me—Annie," I said.

"Of course it is," Walter said.

"I think George is losing his mind," I said. "I think he has gone crazy."

"I always thought he was a bit touched," Walter said.

"I'm serious," I said.

"What did he do?" Walter said. I could see him sitting at the school desk in his small dormitory room still in his underwear, his face gray with sleep, his head leaning slack against the phone.

"He's in love with someone else," I said softly, and though I had intended to tell him all about Maria Bender and her suicide—that George had fallen in love with a dead woman—I discovered suddenly that I could not tell even Walter the truth. I remembered him as he was the day before the wedding, his hair cut short, chin shaved smooth. And I remembered what he told me, although I considered it strange and untrue at the time.

"You and George tiptoe around each other," Walter had said. "Like you're afraid of each other," and he moved his two front fingers across the table like someone walking without sound.

"That's silly," I said. I was convinced then that George and I were perfect for each other, that I would stay married forever.

"Silly but true," Walter had said.

"Oh sure," I said, rolling my eyes, and I had punched Walter in the arm playfully, but certainly harder than I had intended.

Now, because I did not want Walter to be right, and because George's behavior seemed too strange to share, to speak of, I found myself lying to Walter over the phone.

"George is seeing another woman," I told him. "He's sleeping with her behind my back."

There was a long silence; perhaps Walter had actually fallen back to sleep.

"Annie," he said finally in a kind voice. "I know that sounds like insanity to me or you. But a lot of men do it."

I could see Mrs. Nash just outside the office door stamping a price label on the inside cover of a stack of books; it was my job.

"You should have an affair too," Walter recommended. "It's a good cure, and you might have fun." Then he told me he was really half asleep and he would call me later, and we said good-bye.

When I got off the phone, Mrs. Nash told me that I

should not make personal calls from work, and though she did not sound particularly angry I found myself apologizing again and again.

I took Walter's advice and had an affair. It was with a man I knew from work; he organized book-signing parties at the store and his name was Tom. I met him in the evening instead of going to the gym and we spent our time together in a lovely hotel room near the bookstore. The hotel room was larger than my entire apartment, and sometimes I sat there alone after Tom had left, feeling pleased with all that luxurious space. The room was furnished with a large brass bed and there was a silk-covered love seat near the window. The television rose up from a chest at the push of a button. Tom left silly notes and cartoons for me throughout the room, and he surprised me, each time we made love, with a copy of a book signed by its author, wrapped in pretty paper, and done up with a bow. I brought these books home and added them to our already large pile on the windowsill. Some might say I was flaunting my evenings with Tom, but I do not think George even noticed, and the affair lasted for over four months before I told Tom it was through.

"I'm married," I finally said to him on our last evening together. I had never actually said it to him before.

"But not very well," said Tom.

I like to think that I was saddened by what I did or that I felt remorse, but this was only partially true. Perhaps I had finally grown to be like my parents, able to move from one love to another, always looking for available replacements. Or perhaps that need I used to have as a young girl—to do anything not to be alone—had returned. At any rate, I found I was a good liar and took pleasure in my lies the way someone else might take pleasure in a sport they have mastered.

I would also like to think that George gave me just cause for my affair, but this also was not completely true. Shortly after I started seeing Tom, George's infatuation with Maria Bender and her death ceased. It was almost as if it had never been, as if the accident had been caught on a reel of film and George had set the projector into reverse: The train backed up, the lights flickered on, and Maria soared upward through the air, her feet touching the station platform as lightly as a cat's.

George had not gone crazy after all, I realized—or if he had, it was over. In April he sent away for and received a whole slew of new pamphlets in the mail offering him courses on everything from ballroom dancing to creative fathering, and he signed up for some. He went out again at night and came home with new stories about the other students in his classes and jokes the teachers shared about their particular field of interest. George shed whatever grief he had been suffering as if it were a winter coat he had no need for now that the weather had turned warm.

He even threw out the photograph of Maria that he had kept in his wallet all these past weeks.

"I don't know why I ever kept this," he said to me as he tossed the faded newspaper photograph into the trash. "I guess I got a bit carried away."

"I think so," I said.

"I never had death feel so close to me before," George said. "So personal." And he blushed as if he were growing excited again just thinking about it.

"I'm glad it's over," I said, and George came over and put his arms around me.

"I'm sorry, Anne," he said. "So very sorry."

35

It felt good to have his arms around me and I accepted his apology and truly forgave him for the past. But the fear that this could all happen again did not leave, and I did not stop seeing Tom then—he told me no woman had ever made him so happy—and after Tom there was always someone else.

In June, Walter invited George and me to Chicago to watch him graduate from school.

"It's going to be boring," Walter said. "And I want you both to have that pleasure."

"Oh sure," I said.

But George and I were actually looking forward to the trip. We purchased our tickets far in advance and even planned on spending a few extra days in Chicago to relax and see the sights. We had not been away together since the summer before and the prospect of being in a new place, of getting out of our small apartment, made us both a bit giddy. We giggled and planned for the trip like children.

"The hotel is near the lake," George said.

"We'll swan dive into it from the window," I said.

"And I've made reservations for dinner," George said, and he kissed me loudly behind my neck, then nipped me on my ear. "Of course the best dinner is right here," he said.

"You bet," I said.

The day before we were to leave, however, George came home with bad news.

"I can't go," he said. He flung himself on the bed face forward. "My client is settling out of court on Monday and I've got work to prepare."

"What?" I said.

He sat up and looked at me. "I have to work on the case," he said.

"Can't you do it in Chicago?" I said. I sat down next to him on the bed, leaned my head against his shoulder, and wanted to cry. "Can't your client settle it himself?"

"Don't be silly," George said, and then, "I'm sorry." But he did not seem sorry enough.

The next day I left for Chicago alone. I had packed my bags the night before and I left directly from work, taking a taxi to the airport. I got there early and called George at his office to say good-bye, but he was busy and did not have time to talk. After I hung up the phone I went and sat at the gate, waiting for them to call my flight. There were two children there with their mother, waiting for the same plane. They kept asking her in loud high voices when they would leave, and she kept telling them soon, soon, soon.

I realize there are people who fly all the time for business or for pleasure, and when they do they feel as grounded as if they were traveling on a bus or in a car. I do not fly often and I could not explain to such people the sense of freedom I felt in getting on that plane, away from anywhere I had been and from anyone I knew. When we took off, taxiing down the runway and then up into the air, it was as if I had taken flight myself. It was as if the other passengers, the pilot, even the airplane, had suddenly disappeared and I was flying high above the ground alone, surveying the earth like a flattened road map spread out before me.

I pulled off my wedding band and stuffed it into my purse. I loosened my seat belt and ordered a ginger ale from the flight attendant, and I smiled at her and paused a moment before taking it from her hands.

"Do you mind if I turn off the light?" asked the elderly woman who was sitting beside me. Her hair was a soft gray, her face lined, and she was wearing a light brown suit of good-quality wool. Her perfume was sweet and reminded me of the flowers my mother used to plant in a window box when I was young.

"Of course I don't mind," I said, and I watched her reach slowly to turn off the light switch above us, then settle back into her seat, comfortable and at ease with her age.

I stared out the window of the plane, holding my drink in one hand and taking sips from the cool beaded glass. It was dark and I could see only faint traces of white clouds in the sky, and hundreds of tiny lights below me. I thought of George behind one of those many lights. He would be at work still, sitting at the desk in his office, his head cocked to one side, leaning on the palm of his hand. I wondered as I watched him work if he ever pretended not to be married to me, or if he was thinking right now that he was still young enough to start anew, that we were both young. Then I saw the wedding band on his left hand and I saw the look on his face. He looked small from the plane and somewhat sad. I waved to him, but he could not see me up this high in the dark sky and he did not wave back.

"Is anything wrong?" the woman beside me asked.

Startled, I saw that I had dropped my drink into my lap.

"Are you feeling sick, dear?" she said.

"Oh no," I said, and I grinned foolishly as I tried to brush the spilled ice cubes off my skirt; I felt the cold liquid seep through like a shock. "I'm feeling fine," I said.

But the woman smiled and patted my arm as if I were

her granddaughter, young and on an airplane for the first time.

"Don't worry," she said. "We'll be landing soon."

I was not worried. The plane would land in Chicago and later I would return safely to George. I wanted to assure this kind woman beside me that even the most turbulent flights—the shift in wind, a dipping air current, a sudden drop—will pass or be forgiven. It seems the body always forgets.

THE RATING
OF A HURRICANE

There are few who will remember Hurricane Anne.
She was not particularly threatening nor widespread. Not
much more than a long and hard thunderstorm coming in
off the ocean, passing through for the evening and then
leaving as she came. Of course, we did not know this
before she arrived. The people who predict the weather
cautioned those of us who live in and around New York
City to stay indoors for the next eight to twelve hours. The
homes on Long Island must be boarded up tight. They
said the first storm of the year was going to do some real
damage.

Of course, when Anne did no damage of any kind,
instead of being thankful that we were once again spared,
people were angry. They either blamed the weather
forecasters—"I've never known them to be right yet"—or

40

the storm itself—"She calls herself a hurricane. The nerve!" Then everyone promptly forgot about the storm, and the day, and they thought about the future instead.

Nonetheless, I remember Hurricane Anne well. It was on a Sunday; George was working at his office and I sat at home listening to the news on the radio, feeling a certain chill every time I heard them mention Hurricane Anne, as if I were hearing that I had just unwittingly achieved instant notoriety through a winning lottery ticket or a murder.

"That's my name," I said to the radio, although it did not answer back. "They're talking about me."

I tried to read and then to clean the house, but I was easily distracted. I kept running to the window, peering outside and down at the street, looking for people with open umbrellas, yellow rain slickers, faces pressed against their collars. But the rain had not yet begun to fall. It was merely dark and the air was raw with a peculiar smell. I checked the refrigerator and cabinets for food, counting the number of days George and I could last if the storm prevented us from going out. The produce would spoil quickly, but there were boxes of raisins and dates, a bag of walnuts, and four cans of soup that could be rationed. I even called up weather information on the telephone, once every hour, to hear the latest updates. It told me the barometric pressure and the direction and force of the wind. I could hear the menace in the computerized voice. Hurricane Anne was coming, it said. And I was waiting for her, as if, by the very fact that the storm and I had the same name, we were somehow connected, somehow alike.

At noon George called me from his office.

"I'm worried about the beach house," I said to him.

"They're saying Hurricane Anne is going to be the worst storm of the year."

"It's the *first* storm of the year," George said.

"But the house is right on the ocean," I said. "And the storm is coming off the ocean. The Coast Guard in Long Island is on alert."

"Then the house is doomed," said George.

"Really," I said.

"Forget the house," George said. Then he said it would be another few hours before he was home.

"They're warning people to stay indoors," I said to him. "I hope you make it home before the hurricane hits."

"What's a little rain," George said.

"This is not just a little rain," I said.

"I'll be careful," George said and we hung up.

I know there are those who consider my cautious ways a sign of mental disorder. My father once told me if there was nothing left in the world for me to worry about, I would worry about that. And George has told me that no matter how prepared we may believe ourselves to be, life is still going to slap us across the face a few times. There are those who find that slap invigorating; I may even be one of them. Still, I keep my fists in front of my face, my legs moving.

At two o'clock it began to rain, lightly at first and then harder. When I opened the window I felt the damp air enter the room and I could hear the sounds of window wipers in the street and the sound of tires moving across the wet pavement. At three o'clock the phone rang again, and though I was certain it was George telling me he was stuck in his building in a blackout or that the subway home had turned over on the slick track, it was only my father inviting George and me to dinner.

42

"But Hurricane Anne is coming," I said to my father. "We are supposed to stay indoors."

"Hurricane what?" my father said.

"Hurricane Anne," I repeated. "Don't you listen to the weather?"

"Not really," my father said.

I sighed. "It is the worst storm of the year," I said. "We are not supposed to be visiting people for dinner."

"I'm not people, I'm your father," he said. "Besides, Annie, this is important. I have big news I want to tell you about."

"How big?" I said.

"I would not risk your life if I did not feel it was important," my father said.

"Don't make fun of me," I said.

"What's a little rain," my father said. He sounded uncannily like George.

I shrugged. "Okay," I said. "We'll be there."

George and I fought before dinner. In the long haul of marriage it was a fight of little consequence, but these were the kinds of fights George and I excelled at. They were never resolved; one of us merely grew weary first. My brother Walter once told me that George and I fought like this because we were so afraid to deal with the bigger, broader issues.

"Of course, I don't blame you," Walter had said. "I never like to look at anything beyond the reach of my arm. But then, I've got long arms."

"You know nothing about marriage," I'd said to him.

"But I know a lot about fights," said Walter.

This time George and I were fighting about going to my father's for dinner. George was insisting that we take a

43

subway to my father's apartment, while I was in favor of taking a cab.

"But it's pouring out," I said. "And do you know what the winds are blowing at?" I sat on the bed pulling up my stockings and watched as George paced in front of the window. He kept pushing his blond hair back with his hand so that by now it stuck straight up. He chewed on his fingernails. And for a moment we both listened to the strong wind outside.

"I don 't know what the winds are blowing at," George finally said. And, looking at me, "I don't want to know, either."

"Okay, stay ignorant," I said. "But I don't see why you won't take a cab when you know there's a bad storm on its way."

"A cab ride will cost us three times as much as the subway," George said.

"Who really cares?" I said. I stood up, slipped into my shoes, and swung my purse over my shoulder; I was ready to go.

"I care," George said, and he really did. For the last six months he had been making a concerted effort to save money. Not that George had ever been a spendthrift; he had always been slightly cautious, putting a percentage of his paycheck aside for rent, another percentage for monthly expenditures, and still another for his savings account. Only now there was a new fervor to his efforts, he worked more on weekends, he spent less on movies, gifts, clothes.

"I want to change the direction of my career," George told me. In fact, he wanted to leave the large law firm where he worked and enter into a small practice of his own. It was what he had always wanted, I knew. But somewhere in that final year of law school, while happily pursuing me, going out to restaurants and clubs at night,

44

playing house in our small apartment, a high-paying job was offered to him and it could not be refused. Now, George spoke once again of family law, children's rights, and legal aid, as if the words alone were charitable acts.

I agreed, of course, it all sounded noble. But even so, I did not want to go into the subway that night.

"I'm not going out in that storm just to save you a few dollars," I said.

"So throw money away," George said.

"Taking a cab is not throwing money away," I said. "This is throwing money away." I took a five-dollar bill out of my purse and tore it into pieces. I let the pieces fall through my fingers into the trash, feeling vindicated and right.

"You just spent your cab fare home," George said. "Now we will take the subway both ways." And of course we would.

My father was jubilant when we arrived. He hugged me tight in his arms.

"Annie," he said. "You're here!"

"Yes, I'm here," I said.

"And you look wonderful," he said, still hugging me. "Radiant." Then, to Isabelle, "Doesn't she look wonderful?"

Isabelle smiled and nodded in agreement.

Then my father hugged George, too. George stood stiffly, unused to my father's affection.

"Let them come in," Isabelle said. "It's raining."

I had not seen Isabelle in over six months; she did not look well. Her face looked round and heavy and her beautiful blond hair was pulled back tightly off her face. Her eyes seemed misted over, as if she had taken sleeping pills.

"Let them take off their wet things," she said, and my father helped me off with my rain parka.

45

"Wait until you see what Isabelle has cooked for dinner," my father said. "Homemade pasta and this seafood dish. What do you call it?" he said.

"Offer them a drink," Isabelle said to him as if he were a small boy. "And call Yvette in."

So Yvette was here, too. For most of the year she remained in school; I supposed this was one of her vacations, or perhaps the news was so big my father had brought her in just for dinner and she would be shipped away, after the meal was over, with George and me into the midst of the storm.

"We haven't seen you in so long," Isabelle said in her lovely voice as she ushered us into the living room. "And we live so close."

Of course, we had not been invited until now, but I said nothing. Instead I sat down on the couch in the corner and stared across the vast expanse of space that is my father's living room. It is like the rest of the apartment; it reminds me of a gymnasium, it is so spare and large, and hushed, as if everyone were walking around in sneakers. Along one wall there is a window overlooking a green courtyard, and aside from the couch where I sat there was only one other chair, a large armchair my father had bought when he still lived in California. In my father's living room you often felt the need to shout to be heard, and the conversations were usually very loud or nonexistent. I tried to listen for the rain outside, but could not hear it hitting the windows, or even hear the wind. I smiled at Isabelle and admired her dress and then a new painting on the wall. She smiled back at me. Then George smiled, and then we all looked down in embarrassment. I wondered what my father's news might be.

In the past my father had made similar presentations.

There were calls in the middle of the night, telegrams sent, and urgent invitations to meet for lunch or dinner.

"Come quick, Annie," my father would say at these times. "Bring Walter. I've got important news."

Sometimes it was to tell me of a new wife, a new house, or a sudden divorce. Once it was even the death of his mother. But more often it was merely to tell me where he was going on vacation, a painting he had bought, or the new restaurant he had tried out the night before. As if these facts carried no more or less weight than the marriages or the death. They were all equally important because they were about my father. And strangely, Walter and I made them all important, too. We always came when my father called, we were elated at each new marriage, each new home, as if it was the first or the last, although it never was.

My father came into the living room now, carrying a bottle of champagne and five fluted glasses. Behind him was Yvette, looking sullen but somehow prettier than I remembered her. She was wearing a large shirt, the kind that was favored by kids her age, and baggy blue jeans. She had grown her hair long; it lay smooth down her back, and she smiled a genuine smile, large and toothy, when she saw George. If she had been another type of girl, a braver, more assured girl, she might even have kissed George hello. I am sure she wanted to. Instead she blushed and flung herself on the couch beside me.

"Is everyone ready?" my father shouted. He stood tall in the center of the room like a master of ceremonies and held the bottle high in the air. "I have an announcement to make," he said. "That's why George and Annie are here for dinner." Then he began opening the champagne.

47

"Now?" Isabelle said, raising her eyebrows. "I thought you wanted to wait until after dinner."

"I can't wait," said my father. George looked at me. I rolled my eyes. Yvette looked down at the front of her shirt, then at my father with a disapproving sniff.

"I'm not allowed to drink, you know," she said. "I'm not old enough."

"It's a special occasion," my father said. "Like at our wedding."

"My mother said that doesn't matter," Yvette said.

"You can have half a glass," Isabelle said. She was being very quiet; she had sat down in the large full armchair and was resting her head on the broad back of the chair. Her nostrils flared just a bit when the bottle opened with a pop.

My father poured the champagne and handed each of us a glass. Then, holding up his own glass, he proposed a toast.

"Here's to the new member of our family," he said. "Isabelle is going to have a baby."

Isabelle gulped down her glass of champagne. My father clinked his glass against mine, and then against George's and Yvette's.

George smiled and wished my father and Isabelle his warmest congratulations.

"You mean you're pregnant?" Yvette said to her mother. "You're going to have a baby, at your age?"

"Your mother is young," my father said.

I said nothing, but what was one more baby, is what I thought. I did not seriously connect my father's other children to myself; there had been many and they were easily forgotten. I even puzzled sometimes about what made Walter and me different. Why did my father hold on to us, other than the fact that we were first? I know I liked to think that my father merely loved us more, but this was probably a vanity I should have outgrown. Walter once told me it was because we were the only children who refused to leave.

"He'd get rid of us if he could," Walter had said, grinning. "But we keep haunting him. It's like a twilight zone: The Children Who Came to Visit and Never Went Away."

"Grow up," I had said.

It is more likely my father will not let us go because in Walter and me is the semblance of the family he must have once wanted for himself. The family young men imagine when they are first married and do not yet know how quickly love leaves and then comes again. It is a family he may imagine still.

George, who has often expressed concern that my father's personality might be hereditary, has no need to fear. I am not like my father. I no longer live under the illusion that if I keep trying I can make myself the perfect life. Although one of the men I have been with since my wedding was very handsome and the other very rich, I did not think even once of leaving George for them. Walter told me I should keep searching, but he does not understand —there is no one true love, no ideal family, no perfect husband or wife. What George and I have may well be as perfect as it gets. I told Walter this, but he did not believe me.

"Like hell it is, Annie," Walter had said.

My father refilled Isabelle's glass and she swallowed it as if it were a shot of tequila. I thought about their baby, what its family life would be like. And I thought about Yvette. Perhaps after the shock she would actually look forward to having a new sister or brother. They say it is lonely being an only child; she may think they are right. I

knew for certain what George was thinking; he was thinking he did not yet belong in this family, where others
quickly came and went. He would never belong. And
Isabelle looked as if she were thinking that she wanted to
lie down, or jump out the window.

"When is it due?" I asked her.

"Not until January," Isabelle said.

"It could be a New Year's baby," my father said. He
kissed Isabelle on top of her head, then pressed his cheek
against hers. "I'm so happy," he said. Isabelle flinched.

"You don't show a bit yet," I said to her.

"I will soon," she said. "I show early."

"If the baby is born on New Year's Eve you could
win prizes," Yvette said, her thin face lighting up. "They
have contests for the first baby of the new year. It gets its
picture on the front page of the newspaper."

"And you, as the baby's sister, could be in the picture too," said George. Yvette beamed.

"I don't think it's due on the first," Isabelle said.
"Probably closer to the fifteenth."

"As long as it's healthy," George said. He thought
about things like that; we both did.

"Of course it will be healthy," my father said. Then,
nearly leaping across the room, he gave me a quick hug,
and without further thought hugged Yvette too.

"You know who's missing," he said, nuzzling between Yvette and me on the couch. His long legs were
stretched out before him and I noticed he was wearing
brand new running shoes.

"Who?" I said obligingly.

"Walter," Yvette said. "He means Walter."

Walter was still in Chicago. He had finished school
in June and now was involved in various odd jobs. He
edited computer software manuals for two weeks. He

worked in the circulation department of *Playboy* for another six. He even sold Avon products door to door for a while. He had no steady girl and he rarely wrote or called. He never came to visit.

"I wish Walter was here," my father said, somewhat sadly. "He'll be sorry he missed this announcement."

I did not think Walter would be sorry, and although Isabelle showed no sign in her cool face, I do not believe she thought so, either. We were remembering last summer. At least I was certainly remembering it. I thought of the afternoons when Walter and Isabelle would drive off together down the beach, not returning until late. And I thought about the night Walter and I both stayed up in the dark and he told me that yes, this time he was truly in love. But I thought most of all about the day Walter called me from school; it was after the summer was over, and he told me that I had been right, that Isabelle was gone from him forever.

Although it was long past, I calculated the months from the summer, and of course the baby was not Walter's. I assumed, therefore, it was my father's and that the baby was wanted and would be well loved, but I was fearful all the same. It was as if just by the fact that Isabelle and Walter had been together last summer, the baby would come out somehow wrong. It might look like my father and Isabelle, her yellow hair, my father's dark eyes. But it would talk just like Walter.

"What's happening, Annie?" the baby would say in my brother's bright voice. "How's life?" And I shuddered to hear that voice so near and so real.

On the subway ride home that night, George talked again about leaving his job at the firm.

"Don't you think it's time?" he said.

"I don't know," I said. I was thinking about the water on the floor of the subway car. Where was it coming from? It seemed to be pouring in from some hold under the floor of the train. It was creeping nearer and nearer my shoes. It would soon be lapping against them, and then up to soak the leather, and then up further, past my ankles. I imagined the train slowly filling up with water as George and I sat there on our dirty seats. He did not even realize how imminent was our drowning death.

"I've got to get on with my life," George said. "I have to make commitments."

"I'm committed to you," I said.

"You know what I mean," George said. The train jolted for a moment, and I fell against George's shoulder. He shrugged me quickly away.

It was only ten-thirty, but the car was nearly empty. An old man and woman sat across from us, their eyes barely open. And there was a young girl in the corner wearing a tight black leather skirt and short leather boots. The water on the floor had already reached her, and she raised her feet slightly to keep them dry. The only other people on the car were two young men standing near the door and talking softly to each other. Every so often, one of them would look over to the young girl and wink; she ignored him. Once he even looked at me and I smiled at him, though I have been warned not to smile at strangers. The man merely smiled back.

"Where do you think all that water is coming from?" I asked George.

"You're not listening to me," he said. "I'm talking about our future."

"I think the hurricane has hit us down here already," I said.

"It's not a hurricane," George said. "It's a fucking thunderstorm."

"What do you know," I said as if he had made a personal attack on me.

Suddenly the man I had smiled at pushed against the subway door with his feet, slipped, and landed in front of the girl in the leather skirt. Her legs dropped in surprise, her feet landing in the water on the floor.

"That was for you, sugar," the man said, but the girl merely looked at her wet boots and scowled. "Don't ignore me now," he said. The man's friend laughed loudly.

"Go for it," the friend said.

"Get lost," the girl said.

"But I love you more than I've ever loved anyone before," the man said. "You're my only girl. My only love."

For a moment I wondered if the girl actually knew the man, but I realized I was mistaken; they were strangers.

"Cut the shit," the girl said.

"But baby," the man said and he knelt before her, his knees in the dirty water, his hands pressed as if in prayer. "You've just got to be mine."

"Can you believe that guy!" George whispered to me.

"It's kind of nice, don't you think?" I said. "Romantic."

"Sick," George said, and when the old man and woman raised their eyebrows at us, George nodded back.

"I love you, sugar," the man continued. "I want you to have my baby."

But then the train shrieked to a stop and when his friend called out, "Let's go," the man got off his knees, felt his wet pants, and bolted out the subway door. The girl looked after them, then raised her legs once more.

"What a jerk," George said after they had left and

the train slowly started up again. "Harassing that young girl."

"He didn't hurt her," I said.

"He might have," said George.

"I'd be more worried about the water," I said. It was still rising and now actually did lap against my shoes. "We could sink, you know."

"We won't," George said. "Our stop is next."

"It's a good thing," I said, and I splashed through the water on the way to the doors, kicking up bits of Hurricane Anne with each step.

That night George made love to me not once, but three times with extreme fervor.

"Listen to the storm outside," I said to him during a lull. His body felt strong and damp beside me and we listened from our bed to the rain as it hit the window and the street below. The storm seemed to have let up a bit during the night; the wind was no longer shrieking.

"You're my only hurricane," George said. Then, pushing into me again, he said, "I don't want to lose you, Anne. I want you all to myself."

"What?" I said.

"Mine," George said. His body was on top, familiar and intense. "Just mine," he said.

"I am just yours," I said, wishing for a moment that it was true, and believing in some odd way that it was.

"Really," George said, not as a question nor even as a demand. Then he pressed his face against my breasts and I could actually feel tears on his eyelashes and on his cheek.

I am not psychic. But I do believe we are sometimes blessed with slight premonitions. I was at work at the bookstore when the phone rang and I knew before Mrs. Nash answered it that it would be for me and that it would be Isabelle. I do not know how I knew this; Isabelle has never called to invite me for lunch before, and the phone rings often in the bookstore and is rarely for me. But I did know, and if I had thought about it I might even have known why.

We met at a small French restaurant only a few blocks from the bookstore. They knew Isabelle there and gave us a good table in the corner and the maître d' whispered something in Isabelle's ear that made her smile.

Isabelle ordered for both of us in French, while I sat there rolling my napkin up and down my leg, first into a tight roll, then loose, then up tight again. There was wine which the waiter brought and Isabelle directed him to pour our glasses to the top. Then she proposed a toast.

"There have been a lot of toasts recently," I said.

"Here's to you and me," Isabelle said. "Two women of passion."

It was then that I realized Isabelle had already been drinking. There was a certain looseness to her words, a redness to her eyes. She must have started early; it was just noon.

Our glasses touched and we both drank nearly half our wine before we spoke again.

"I'm leaving your father," Isabelle said as she placed her glass down. "I'm in love with someone else. Someone you don't know," she added wisely.

Although the meaning was clear, I did not at first understand what Isabelle was saying. I thought perhaps she was going on a trip, or that it had something to do with the baby.

"I'm telling you first," Isabelle continued, "because I

55

sensed you would understand. You understand what a woman will do for love."

The waiter came with our salads and I had time to think about what Isabelle was telling me. She was leaving my father. She was seeing someone else.

"I don't understand," I said.

Isabelle took a small bite of her salad. I noticed her nails were perfectly manicured and polished. Her hands were smooth and graceful. I could see the tendons underneath the skin as she clasped her fork and then set it down.

"You're an unhappy woman," Isabelle said. "I saw it the night you were over for dinner."

"I'm not unhappy," I said.

"Would you like some more wine?" It was the waiter standing at my side, the bottle poised above my glass.

I nodded to him and he refilled both our glasses.

"I know you are not faithful to George," Isabelle said, offering me the bread in the center of the table. "They make the bread themselves," she said. "It's quite good."

"I am faithful," I said, but I was like a child caught in a lie. I blushed and bit my lip. I felt very young all of a sudden, as if I were a little girl playing dress-up in an elegant restaurant. My feet did not touch the floor. The wine was making me ill.

"Not that I blame you," Isabelle said. "He's always seemed a bit off to me. The night of your wedding he gave me a lecture on being an American, of all things."

"You barely know George," I said.

Isabelle shrugged.

"In fact everything you're saying is wrong," I continued, and I wished that it all were. But Isabelle *was* wrong about one thing; it was not just passion I was after, but something else, something quieter and more enduring. I did not know what it was.

I looked squarely now at Isabelle. "I would never leave George," I said. My voice was too loud for the small restaurant and people turned toward our table. Just then the waiter came by with our food and he raised his eyebrows as he placed my plate before me. He looked like my father does when I disappoint him in some way.

"Lower your voice," Isabelle said.

"Don't worry," I said. "I'm leaving."

"Anne," Isabelle said. She reached over and took my arm, not allowing me to rise from the table. "You know as well as I do that if I didn't leave your father he would eventually leave me. His track record speaks for itself."

"And what about the baby?" I said.

"It's not his," Isabelle answered, although that was not the question I had asked.

I shook my head, and rose once again to leave.

"Anne," Isabelle said. "Don't worry." Then in that same low voice she asked me to please stay, to have lunch with her as planned. "You'll enjoy the food here," she said. "Have lunch with me. I wish you would."

So I did stay for lunch; I was hungry, Isabelle was persuasive, and for some reason I still wanted her to like me, to share confidences with me in the future. She talked about babies and the town where she was born. She had been named after her father's lover, she told me. I talked about Hurricane Anne.

"It only received a rating of one out of five on the hurricane scale," I told Isabelle.

"What won't they rate these days," she said.

"They had predicted a three," I said.

"I'm sure it's all guesswork," Isabelle said.

Upon leaving the restaurant, the maître d' touched

my chin with the tips of his fingers. "I hope you'll come back soon," he said to me. "It's such a pleasure. Such a beautiful girl."

"He likes you," Isabelle whispered to me. "He told me so."

"That's hardly enough," I said, swinging out of the dark restaurant into the bright day.

"That's exactly what I've been trying to tell you," Isabelle said. "You need some passion." Then we parted company in the street.

My lunch hour was more than over, but I did not want to go back to work. I thought of calling my father and warning him about Isabelle, but I realized that was silly; he would learn soon enough. And I thought of calling Walter, telling him what a fool he had been last summer, to fall in love with a woman like that. But Isabelle was not without her charms, and my brother was still young. Instead, I walked two blocks over to an office courtyard where I sometimes had lunch when the weather was nice. It was shaded with small trees, and vendors surrounded the courtyard selling pretzels and frozen yogurt and sweet-smelling meat on a stick. There was only one unoccupied bench left when I arrived, and I sat down and kicked off my shoes. I watched the people walk by—women in high heels, men in business suits—all with somewhere to go.

The air smelled good, for the city, still brisk and clean from all the rain, and the buildings seemed particularly bright, as if they had been recently polished by a troupe of trapeze artists swinging their dustcloths a hundred stories above the ground. Now the buildings gleamed in the sun, tall and imposing, and, though more transient than the vistas we find in nature, I found the buildings no less amazing.

"I am not unhappy," I suddenly said out loud, this time with feeling, although Isabelle was no longer there to hear me or be convinced. "Not unhappy at all," I said.

A man wearing a Yankees cap was walking by and he grinned at me. "Glad to hear it," he said.

I grinned back, certain now that I was still unscathed. Still spared. In fact, that is what I thought as I walked back to work, and I felt it still as I unboxed books at the store, placed them by subject and author on the shelves. And this gladness, as I came to call it, stayed on with me, even after I returned home that night.

IT IS THE LITTLE
THINGS IN LIFE

W‍e got the call early on a Sunday morning and we argued about who would answer it, although in our apartment the telephone was never far from where you might be. I was making breakfast at the stove and George was looking through the newspaper, front to back, every page. The telephone rang eleven times before George picked it up.

It was his mother from New Hampshire. George's father had died of a heart attack during the night. When his mother woke up, her husband was dead in the space beside her.

I do not much remember the events immediately following that call, except that I slid my half-cooked omelet down the sink and felt particularly angry at the waste of food. I think George told me his father was only fifty-five and had no right to die so young. Then I suppose we did what countless others have done in a similar situation—called the airline, packed our bags, and watered our plants on the way out the door—we left to mourn the dead.

I told George what my father had taught me, that it is not the large events, like birth and like death, that shape our lives, but the small distinct memories we carry with us like an added appendage—an extra arm, a third ear.

"Memories make you behave in the oddest ways," my father once said to Walter and me. It was during dinner and we had been complaining to him right up through dessert, as if eating together were some tedious chore we were made to perform free of charge. Walter wanted to meet his friends downtown, he told my father, and I was waiting for some boy to call. He certainly would not call if I were eating dinner with my father.

"It is the little things in life that change you," my father continued, and then, because he was afraid Walter and I were not listening, he added, "One day you will remember this dinner and it will affect you in some profound way."

I rolled my eyes and Walter tossed his napkin in the air and bolted from the table. Only now I see that my father was right. Walter and I both remember that dinner; I was thirteen, Walter twelve, and my father had made spaghetti and a marinara sauce that tasted too much of tomatoes. To this day we believe what we were told during that meal; it is the seemingly small memories—the summer it was so hot Walter and I made black animals out of the melted tar in the street, the last Christmas tree we decorated with my mother at home, the night Walter and I identified twenty-six constellations in a December sky—that make us who we are.

George grew up with no such advice and he disagreed. He considered his father's death the most traumatic and important event in his life.

"But there's nothing you can do about your father dying," I have told him over and over.

"But I will always wish that I could," George said.

George's parents owned a home in southern New Hampshire near the university where his father taught mathematics for nearly twenty years. We had visited them only once before, when we first married, and I had brought with me a box of beautifully wrapped Swiss chocolates as a gift.

"You shouldn't have wasted your money," George's father said to me when I handed him the box of candy.

"Neither of us eats sweets, dear," his mother said.

I looked at George for help but he ignored me, or perhaps he didn't notice.

"You bring them back home with you," his mother said, and she took the chocolates from her husband and urged them back into my arms.

"Oh really," I said. "Surely you'll eat them someday."

"No," his mother said. "We won't."

They were strange quiet people that weekend we were there. His mother, who was very active in an animal humane society, worked on a speech she was to deliver the following week. She read it aloud to us after dinner and it was obvious by the way she spoke of these cruelties that she felt a great deal for the mistreated animals of the world, but when I asked her about the organization she grew silent.

"We try to save animals," she told me in a flat voice, and that was all.

George's father sat in his study most of the weekend

correcting exams and we tiptoed around, fearful of disturbing him. Late Saturday afternoon, though, he emerged from his room dressed in jeans and an old sweater and he herded George and me outside to watch him chop wood. It was a huge pile of wood, but George's father had no difficulty splitting the logs. He did not talk as he swung the axe, but breathed heavily in the cool air. Only later, as George and I stacked the wood for him, did he speak a little—about his new class of students, about last year's winter, and once about George's younger sister, Virginia.

"She is changed," he told us, "since she moved to California. She is greatly changed."

We had not been back to their home in New Hampshire since, nor had we been invited. George rarely spoke of his parents and they never phoned or wrote.

"How come you and your parents are so distant from each other?" I once asked him.

"We're not," George said. "We all love each other very much." I suppose in their own way they did.

During the flight to Boston, George pretended we were not together, that our seating arrangement was unexpected and not by choice. He read the airline magazine and I watched the clouds move by outside the window. When the flight attendant offered us drinks, we each paid for our own separately, and when we landed George strode off without me, leaving me to locate my luggage by myself.

"George," I called, running after him, but he would not turn around.

Perhaps his grief was too much for him to share, or perhaps it was because he still did not regard me as a member of his family, not really entitled to be there at all. At any rate, we drove in our rented car for over an hour before he would speak. I investigated the glove compartment for maps and traced our route with my finger, and George drove steadily, holding the wheel, staring out at the road.

We were passing small farms now and the road narrowed and curved, and I knew we were getting closer to the home where George had grown up. I tried to remember what his parents looked like, or things they had said, but I could remember neither. I tried to imagine what the funeral would be like, who would be there, what we would say. I did not remember going to any funerals with my own family, and I did not know how we behaved. I saw us, though, all together in my father's apartment—Walter and Isabelle and Yvette, and of course the cousins, uncles, and aunts who had always surrounded us at holidays, graduation ceremonies, and the like. We were all much too loud for the large hollow rooms of my father's apartment and the noise was deafening, yet we kept bumping into each other as if stuffed into a hall closet. My father told us stories about when we were young, Walter and my oldest cousin, Steve, drank far too much and told dirty jokes to the youngest ones. We talked about everything but death. There was nothing frightening about this funeral with my family; it was all as familiar and ritualized as Christmas.

Suddenly, for the first time since we had left New York, George turned to me. "I wish I could have given my father a grandchild before he died," he said. "My father once told me that would be his greatest pleasure in the world. He loved being a father. It was the best time of his life—when Virginia and I were young."

"I never knew that," I said. "You never told me."

George ignored me. "My mother wants a grandchild too," he said. "And now it's too late."

64

"It's not too late," I said to George, and I closed the glove compartment with a click. "We can still have a baby."

"Anne, you don't understand," George said. "My father's dead. And then I'll be dead. Dead, dead, dead," he repeated, sounding like a record with a skip.

I thought he was going to cry, but he didn't. Instead he rested his head on top of the steering wheel and let go of it with his hands. The car veered for an instant onto the other side of the road and I screamed.

"Watch the road," I said.

"Go to hell," George said, but before we could crash he lifted his head and took hold of the steering wheel once more.

George's parents' house was much like the other houses on the block. Built at the same time, it was a small split-level with white aluminum siding and black shutters, but because it was the house where George grew up I saw what made it different. George's sister, Virginia, had sent a brilliant blue hammock from California and it swung between two large oak trees. There was an elaborate homemade bird feeder where even now sparrows were feeding. And there was a row of hemlocks that George and his father planted the year before George left for law school. The hemlocks were tall now and George pointed them out to me as we entered the house.

"I wish my father was here to see how tall they've grown," George said.

"He saw them," I said.

"Not with me," said George.

Inside the house was quiet, as if not only his father had died, but the house itself. The carpeted stairway, the furniture and draperies, even the refrigerator and stove, alone in the kitchen, had all fallen numb and silent from a

65

heart attack during the night. George's mother was asleep upstairs in her room, and Virginia had not yet arrived from San Francisco. His only other living relative, his aunt Polly, was sitting on the couch in the living room. She kissed George very lightly hello, and shook my hand.

"We're glad you both could make it," she said.

"Of course we made it," I said.

Then she took George's hands between her own and held them there, looking into his eyes. I coughed uncomfortably, but George said nothing. Perhaps he was used to this kind of behavior.

"You will never guess what has happened," Polly finally said with effort. She was still holding onto George's hands.

I thought she was referring to the death of George's father, and I wondered what else she would think we would be there for, at this hour, in this mood. But Polly's news was something quite different. It involved a hand-delivered letter George's mother had received only that afternoon from one of her husband's graduate students—a boy named Larry Populace. Evidently, Larry, who had studied closely with George's father for three years and even worked as his teaching assistant for the last six months, felt compelled to break his silence after learning about the death.

"I don't know why he told us now," Polly said. "When it's too late."

"Was he having an affair?" George guessed, and I thought immediately of my own affairs. Would the men I had slept with during my marriage write George letters after my death? "Your wife slept with us," the letters would say. "She barely mentioned you." George would scatter these letters over my grave without shedding a tear, and I would deserve it.

"Much worse," said Polly, her thin body visibly trembling. "He exposed himself in class. The letter said that—expose."

I almost giggled, although it was not really funny— the thought of George's father standing before his graduate class in mathematics pulling his trousers down to his ankles. Perhaps it was just another annoying idiosyncracy a person might pick up after teaching for so many years, like wiping chalk off on the front of a shirt, or tapping a pencil as if it were a drumstick.

"Exposed himself?" George said. "Like some kind of pervert?"

Polly finally let go of George's hands and sat back down on the couch. She held her face in her hands. "Of course, we're not sure it's true," she said. "But the letter itself was upsetting enough."

"Probably Larry is just some student Dad failed," George said. "Nothing true about it."

"Polly said he was your father's teaching assistant," I said, and they both stared at me as if I had intruded upon their private conversation. I suppose in a way I had.

"I'm sure he's lying," George said.

"Your mother is not so sure," Polly said, and she pulled the letter from the pocket of her skirt and held it out to George for him to read.

Larry's letter was typed and obviously much thought out. Its intention was not to shock, but rather to set the record straight, as if he felt it important that a man's life be documented properly after his death.

It had been going on for over a year, we learned. Some students transferred out of his class, while others, I imagined, laughed at him. Still others, like Larry, kept quiet because they respected him and hoped it would pass.

"There was nothing lewd about his actions," wrote Larry in his letter. "It was as if he could not help himself."

"How could he not help himself?" George said.

"We don't know," Polly said as if George had expected a reply. "We imagine he just cracked in some way."

"It did not affect his teaching," Larry Populace concluded. "He was an excellent mathematician and an inspiring teacher at all times."

"Even when he was flashing in front of his students," said George.

"Go see your mother," Polly said. "She has been waiting for you upstairs. She is most upset."

I was not sure which upset her more, the letter or her husband's death. I am not sure that it mattered.

Polly showed me to George's old bedroom, where we would be staying. There were two twin beds, and on the bookshelf a model pirate's ship that George had built as a young boy. There were also numerous trophies that he had won in sports events—first-place baseball and soccer teams for three years, a second place for the butterfly in a swim meet and another first the following year, various varsity letters. There was even a trophy, the largest, for most valuable baseball player his senior year in high school. It was strange that nothing had come from all of this. Although George was still athletic, he no longer participated in team sports or events.

"I'm not like you," George once told me when I asked him why he no longer played baseball, or even swam. "I can put things behind me."

"But it was such a large part of your life," I said. "And you were so good."

"Yes, I was," George had said, not at all sadly. "I

68

never do things half-assed." Then he looked at me with those steady eyes, as if to imply that there were many things I had not done completely, or even very well.

Now I undressed and lay down on one of the narrow beds, staring out into the unfamiliar room. I tried to hear what George and his mother were saying next door, but their voices were just a hum in my ear. I listened for the sound of Virginia's arrival; her flight was expected late that night. I had only met her once, at the wedding. She looked like George, blond and tall, healthy, but she was louder and more demonstrative. She had hugged me when we met.

"I'm glad you're marrying George," she had said as she held me. "You don't seem at all like him."

"We're very similar," I protested. "That's why we're getting married."

"No, he's just like his father," Virginia said. "Two peas in a pod."

She had danced with all the men at the wedding, including the man who had come with her from California. He was feminine-looking and well dressed. He spoke to no one. Every once in a while Virginia left the dance floor and wandered over to me.

"This is really funny, you know," she said. "Strange, but really funny."

George never did come to bed that night, and in the morning I found him and his mother and his Aunt Polly sitting around the breakfast table together. They were talking about the arrangements for the funeral, which was to be held that afternoon. Polly said she would continue making the appropriate calls and George said he would go over to the funeral home that morning and check on the arrangements there. When I asked what I could do to help, they all looked at me.

"Anne, dear," his mother said kindly, "you're a guest."

George served me breakfast and the three of them continued talking among themselves. I wondered if this was how George felt when he was with my family, like an eavesdropper or a Peeping Tom, someone whose actions were tolerated, but certainly not well approved.

As I ate the eggs and toast that George had prepared I learned that Virginia had never arrived.

"Perhaps she missed her flight," I offered.

"Anne," George said, "we talked to Virginia. She told us she wasn't coming."

"I never liked her," Polly said. "Even if she is my own niece."

"She told my mother she couldn't afford the flight," George said to me. "She called us up this morning to tell us that."

"She never cared a hoot about anyone but herself," Polly said.

"She and her father were always so close," George's mother said. "It's such a shame." George's mother was dressed in a beige skirt and white silk blouse. Her hair was cut short and neat. Although her face was made up, you could tell she had been crying. I realized I did not know her, but it was not difficult to imagine what she was feeling. I was sure she was thinking that life was dealing her a lot of troubles in the last forty-eight hours, troubles not so clearly defined as the ones that afflicted the animals she worked so hard to save.

"Why don't we help her with the flight," I whispered to George.

"It's too late, Anne," George said. "She couldn't make it in time now."

"But it's her father's funeral," I said.

"You don't understand, do you?" George said.

"How could she, dear?" George's mother said. "How could she?"

I went with George to the funeral home to visit his father. I had never seen a dead person before and I was surprised to find that instead of being macabre or sad, the sight left me feeling nothing at all. The man in the funeral home looked not at all the way I had remembered George's father; he did not look human, nor even like one of those wax figures in a museum, which is how dead people always appeared to me in the movies or on television. He looked instead like a man who had never lived.

"Do you want to be alone with him?" I asked George.

"No," he said. "I really don't."

I held his hand and we stood there for quite a while, not really looking at George's father, but not really looking at anything else.

"I never admired my father the way you admire yours," George said to me at one point. "And after that letter yesterday—" George's voice broke, but he continued to hold tightly onto my hand.

"It doesn't change who he was," I said.

"That's just the point," George said. "I never thought he was much, anyway." Then George started to cry. I helped him to a couch that was outside in the hall, and we both sat down while I held him and would not let him go.

Many people showed up for the funeral that afternoon. We milled around outside in the cold New Hampshire air, stamping our feet and occasionally looking north toward the White Mountains. People came up to George's mother one by one or in pairs, and I heard someone ask where Virginia was.

"Her plane is greatly delayed," George's mother said without skipping a beat.

71

There was a small group from the animal humane society, each wearing a button on their lapel with the face of an unrecognizable breed of dog, and there was another whole contingent from the university—students and faculty, talking quietly among themselves, some even crying. The head of the mathematics department came over to George and me to offer his condolences.

"Your father was a very fine mathematician and a grand teacher," the man said. "We will all miss him."

"I don't believe him," George said to me under his breath. "Do you?"

After him there followed a young girl who had been a student of George's father.

"He was my favorite teacher," she said. "I always hated math until I had your father. He made it fun." I wondered if she had been in any of Larry Populace's classes, if *that* had made math fun. I even looked for Larry, not that I would have recognized him if I saw him. I thought I knew what he looked like, though, a serious graduate student with a nervous twitch in his eye and a bulge in his back pocket from carrying a calculator, the kind of person who could understand another man's shortcomings but could not excuse them.

In the university chapel, the four of us—Polly, George, his mother, and I—sat in the front row, while the minister spoke solemnly of a life cut short too soon. It was a lovely chapel, small and warm. The wooden pews had been rubbed smooth from use, and the carpeting was worn, but it was comforting to be among so many people and to hear the voice of the minister, even-paced and sane.

George, sitting beside me, shifted in his seat to look at the faces of the people behind us. "This is the church we used to go to when I was growing up," he whispered to me. "We would all go together, Virginia and me and my parents. I used to fall asleep."

"Shh," Aunt Polly said.

George ignored her. "My parents thought it was important for us to go together to pray," he said. "Our prayers had more power that way, my father told me."

"I think he was right," I said, although except for weddings, no one in my family attended church. My father told Walter and me when we were young that religion was a private affair.

"Best kept behind closed doors," my father had said. "Best done alone."

"He said that by staying together we could stay strong," George continued, and then, "He must be terribly sad that Virginia is not here."

"I'm sad," I said.

"Shh," Polly said again.

After the short sermon, a man rose to play the organ; it was a beautiful hymn, slow and melancholy. I closed my eyes and listened to the music; it made me feel strange and alone. I wished that George's father had never died, and then I missed my own father. I prayed that he was healthy and well, and then I imagined him there beside me.

"I want more than this when I die," my father was saying to me. "Do it right for me when I'm gone, Anne, do it right."

Walter was there, too, only it didn't look like Walter. He was dressed up like a minister in a robe and black shoes, and as the organ continued to play Walter walked up to the front of the chapel.

"What are you doing?" I said, but he did not hear me.

Instead, he rose to the pulpit and threw his arms up to the air. "I am here to tell the sad story of a man gone wrong,'' Walter shouted like a revivalist preacher. The people in the pews shouted back, "Amen."

"It's the tragic story of a flasher," Walter continued. "A man no one tried to save."

The crowd of people began to sway.

"You all knew, but no one spoke up," Walter shouted to us. "Pray to God for his forgiveness."

"That's my son," my father said.

Then the head of the math department raised his hands above his head. "He had been with us so long we looked the other way," the man said. "I pray to Jesus."

"He made it fun," the young girl student shouted from the back. "I pray for my redemption."

The organ music was rising to a crescendo. The people in the pews prayed and chanted.

Then Larry Populace was standing up. He was wearing glasses, but he threw them out to the crowd. "I see it all clearly now," he exclaimed. "He was a tortured mathematician. I should have said something sooner. Now it's too late. Too late to save him."

"We have all killed him," said Walter.

"Your brother has a point," my father was saying beside me.

And the organ music grew louder and louder.

Suddenly I felt George nudging my arm. "Anne," he said.

"I'm just listening to the music," I said. I opened my eyes to the sight of people walking slowly past the closed coffin. No one was shouting; they were all silently mouthing their prayers.

"But what are you thinking about?" George said.

"I was thinking about your father," I said.

"I can't stop thinking about him, either," George said.

*   *   *

That night I called my father to ask him if he would pick up George and me at the airport. We would be leaving the next morning and would arrive in New York around noon. Could he be there?

"Of course," my father said to me over the phone. And, agreeably, "Anything at all." Since Isabelle's departure he was eager to be of service, anxious to show me he was still a good man, that the fault was not his own. Then he asked, "How is George taking it all?"

"He's getting through," I said. "But it sure is strange."

"Don't let it upset you, Annie," my father said. "Death happens all the time."

"But I don't think it happens quite like this," I said. I hung up the phone.

I will always remember what took place next; it is like the sight of dead Christmas trees left along the curb or a pumpkin smashed on Halloween. It was a mother and son sitting at a familiar kitchen table. The son taps his fingers. The mother brushes some crumbs into the palm of her hand. They are not talking, but each is staring horrified at the one empty seat, as if the dead father and husband were still sitting there. He is waiting for dinner, his body lifeless and decaying.

"Come in, dear," George's mother said when she saw me, and I joined them in the kitchen. I could hear Polly in the living room where she was entertaining some neighbors who had come to pay their respects; someone laughed and then Polly's shrill laugh followed.

"We were just talking about you," George said, and he poured me a cup of coffee from the pot on the table, although it was long cold, and then looked not at me, but back at the empty chair with that same eerie expression on his face.

"Anne," he finally said. "My mother has asked me to stay here awhile. Just until things get settled down." He said it as if his mother had asked only to borrow a book from him or a few dollars to see her through payday.

"What's awhile?" I said.

"A month, maybe two," George said. "I can take a leave of absence from the office." He took my hand, and quickly, as if it were burning cold, let it go. George's mother looked down at the front of her dress and said nothing.

"That's not awhile," I said.

"I've got to take care of my family now," George said.

"I'm your family," I said, but I was not at all sure.

"You know what I mean," George said.

"No," I said. "I don't."

"I have no one, dear," his mother said. Then she opened her clasped hands as if to show me nothing, no one.

"You have Polly," I said.

"That's like having no one," said George.

"I don't want to be alone, either," I said. "I want you with me." I was whining now, like a young child, and I could feel George pulling away.

"Please, Anne," he said. "I'm sorry."

"No, I'm sorry," I said. And I suppose I realized then that I would be going home alone.

George's stay in New Hampshire, though, was not as long as he had planned. In less than two weeks he flew back to me in New York and was once again dreaming about some perfect distant future, working Saturdays and Sundays, attending classes at night. He never really explained to me what happened—whether he and his mother had a fight, or whether he realized, after the shock of his father's death had dimmed, that as my husband his place was with me.

"I missed you," was all he said as we lay together in bed his first night back in New York.

"Not as much as I missed you," I said.

George held me in his arms and I felt his breath on my neck and the movement of his body in the dark. We did not talk for a long while.

"I thought about families while I was gone," George finally said.

"You did?" I said.

"I keep thinking there is supposed to be something more," George said. "To families, I mean."

"Like what?" I said. The only family I knew well was my own; it seemed plenty enough for me.

"I don't know, Anne," George said. "Just not like this."

I knew what he meant, but instead kissed his forehead, then his cheek. "I don't think this is so bad," I said, kissing his lips, but if George agreed I do not know. He curled his legs around mine, hushed me with his finger, closed his eyes. And if that night he dreamed, I am sure it was for us both.

THE THANKSGIVING
BIRD

T hree weeks before Thanksgiving, Walter and I inherited a windfall. Uncle Theodore, my mother's only brother, died earlier than expected, leaving Walter and me each a quarter of a million dollars. A third would be taken out in taxes, we were promptly informed, but it was still a sizable amount and if invested wisely might even change our fortune.

"Why did he leave it to you?" George asked. His training as an attorney had prepared him to ask the right questions. George takes nothing for granted, leaves no stones unturned.

"He had no wife, no children," I said. That was about all I knew of my uncle Theodore, a lifetime bachelor who had made a lot of money in New York real estate. I had met him once or twice at Christmas before my mother left us. Uncle Theodore, well-dressed, with platinum blond hair, had sat awkwardly in the corner of our living room, watching us open our Christmas gifts as if we were aliens performing some strange and slightly perverse ritual or rite of passage. Of course, he brought presents for us, too, but they were always grossly wrong—gifts for a child much younger or older. A Wedgewood china dish one year for me, a leather manicure set for five-year-old Walter.

"And Theodore never cared for my mother," I added. This was also something I had picked up quite young. My mother used to say to my father that her brother was homosexual though he would never admit it. I sensed there was something else between them, that they resented each other from some long-ago event I would never hear about. When she and Theodore were together they spoke in short, clipped sentences and my mother always lavished too much praise on his endeavors, something she only did with people she despised.

"That's a good deal of money you've just inherited," George said. We were still sitting at the dinner table, although we had finished eating almost an hour ago. The news had rendered us each inert. George stirred the remains of his tea. I had torn a napkin into shreds. "I wonder what Walter will do with his share," George said.

Of course, he was really wondering what I would do with my money. Since his father's death George had all at once given up talk of leaving his law firm in the city.

"Another plan wasted, gone," he had told me, and also that dreams so remote no longer seemed possible to him, and certainly not mature. Instead, with that same sort of obsessive quality, he now spoke of moving out of our tiny studio apartment into someplace larger, or even buying a house in New Jersey or Connecticut. He had some money saved and on weekends he looked at the real estate section in the paper. I might even have joined him in his search, if he were doing it for us. But George did it because he wanted children.

"I realize since my father died," George explained to me, "that the way to really help the world is by having children."

He had begun to badger me weekly for a child, and could not understand why I refused.

"Is it the money?" he sometimes asked. "Don't you like children?" And, more often, "Is it me?"

"I don't know," I always answered, though of course I did.

I rolled the shreds of the napkin into a ball and placed it on my empty plate. There had already been the other men and now I was seeing someone new. His name was Arlo and he played the drums in a band. Although I had not yet considered leaving George for any of these men, I wondered for a moment if Uncle Theodore's money might change my mind—send me on a trip or into divorce. More likely, however, it was not enough money to seriously change my life, not enough to persuade me to have a child or even quit my job.

"Walter will move back east with his share of the money," I said with the conviction that comes from growing up close to a sibling. "And he will buy lavish gifts for whatever girl he's currently dating."

"Sounds like a wise investment," George said.

"It's his money," I said.

Then we sat there together for a long time without saying a word. I wondered what my father would say, if it would be a comfort knowing he would no longer be called to bail Walter and me out of our none-too-few financial jams, if he would finally consider us provided for. Or perhaps he would feel jealous, that our good fortune should come from my mother's side.

George tapped my shoulder. "You there?" he asked. "Or dreaming of your wealth?"

"Of course I'm here," I said.

"So what are you going to do with your windfall?" he asked. I knew he was trying to sound nonchalant, but even when George is being casual there is a formality to his way of speaking, a studied air.

"I'm going to have an enormous Thanksgiving feast," I said. "The kind we used to have when I was a little girl."

"I don't think that will use your entire fortune," George said.

"Probably not," I said. "But it's a start."

Thanksgiving has always been my favorite holiday. I reason it is a day we are asked to do only what we should be doing all the days of the year—giving thanks for what we have.

When my mother was still living with us, she used to make a large Thanksgiving feast every year. She would order the turkey months in advance and it would be delivered early in the morning, freshly plucked and ready to be stuffed with her famous chestnut and sausage stuffing. Walter and I would kneel on chairs at the kitchen table chopping walnuts for the cranberry sauce and apples and pears for pie. My father would place a case of champagne out on the terrace to keep it cool until the guests arrived. Sometimes there was a goose in addition to the turkey; my mother had invited new friends or business acquaintances and we would add another leaf to the already large dining room table. We would sit together, strangers and family alike, and although we were not religious by nature, my father would give a short blessing before the feast, thanking God for what we had and what we might receive in the future. Then all of us at the table would echo amen.

After my mother left us, Thanksgiving became much more haphazard. Two of my father's wives were terrible cooks and they ordered Thanksgiving dinner from a local carterer who delivered only enough food for the one meal—one small turkey, one bowl of canned cranberry sauce, a pumpkin pie in a metal tin. There were never any leftovers and I was jealous of the children at school eating their lunches of turkey and stuffing sandwiches, ached as I listened to them complain that there would be one just like it tomorrow.

Although Isabelle and my father had only separated for a few months, I had heard they were now back together. Even so, Isabelle had never prepared our Thanksgiving meal and would certainly not start now. She had lived most of her life in New York City, but was French by birth and asserted this fact at odd times. Our big family holiday was now Christmas, and despite the presents and the tree and the feast of goose and ham which Isabelle did most adeptly prepare, it did not compare to my memory of Thanksgiving.

I planned my guest list carefully. My father and Isabelle, of course, and Yvette. Walter would come in from Chicago. And in a moment of generosity I decided to invite George's mother in New Hampshire. We had not seen her since her husband's death, but George called her every second Sunday and I could tell from the tone of his slow, patient voice that it was a difficult call. There were friends I thought of inviting, too—a woman from work who lived alone with her cat, and a man I had known since college who met me sometimes at the gym for racketball or squash. At the last minute, however, both friends were crossed off the list. The man's presence would only embarrass George and the woman was an extremely vocal dieter. Besides, there really was not enough room in the apartment for them both.

As it turned out I could have invited them, as well as George's boss and the man in the corner shop who gave me free coffee with my Danish in the morning. My father and a very pregnant Isabelle were spending a reconciliatory Thanksgiving week in St. John's sunning on the beach. They sounded happy when I spoke to them, and Isabelle's return was never explained. Perhaps the other man had left her or had turned out to be something other than expected. Or perhaps it was because my father had agreed to raise the soon-to-be-born child as his own.

"But what does it matter?" my father said to me when I asked. "She's my wife again."

Although I thought that with her mother gone Yvette might be spending Thanksgiving alone at school and might enjoy a dinner with family, I discovered she too was busy and would be in California with her father. Even George's mother called to give her regrets. It was kind of me to ask, she told me, but it was a critical time at the animal shelter where she worked. She couldn't possibly leave now.

So only Walter was to come. He was excited over the phone and asked if he could bring his friend Allegra.

"She's a real dream," Walter said.

"I'll bet," I said.

"She is the one," Walter said.

"Sounds it," I said.

Then we talked a bit about the money, avoiding the subject of where it came from or where it was really going to go.

"Thanksgiving dinner," said Walter finally. "Doesn't that beat it all."

"I guess it does," I said, and I felt giddy and proud.

Two days after I received news of my inheritance, I took an afternoon off from my work at the bookstore to be with Arlo. Arlo shared a loft in Soho with his sister, Irene. She worked as a door guard at one of the newest and hottest after-hours clubs in the city. She was the person who selected who would be allowed to enter, who would be left to stand in the dark waving their hands like game show contestants, "Pick me, pick me."

"I try not to be a snob about it," Irene once told me. "But you should see some of the people who want to get into the club. Lower than dog shit," she said.

Arlo often encouraged me to join him at the club some night.

"There are lots of celebrities there. I danced with Jerry Hall one night," he told me. "And Irene would have you comped all the way into the morning."

"Wow," I said. But I always turned him down. "I have a husband," I would remind him. "He looks for me at night."

We never called George by name.

Arlo's sister was sleeping when I arrived. Her long black hair was like a sash across her face and she was wearing some kind of oriental outfit. Both of her arms clutched at her pillow.

Arlo was in the kitchen, or what they called the kitchen. It was actually just an alcove with a small refrigerator and a stove. There was no oven. Arlo was uncapping a beer and he offered me one as I entered. I shook my head no.

Arlo and I had been seeing each other for almost three months. I thought he was the best-looking man I had seen during my marriage. His eyes were so brown they were opaque and reflected nothing. I had never seen eyes like his and sometimes when he was sleeping I woke him up to look at his eyes. He also had well-developed arm muscles—I'd seen him flex in front of the mirror—that he claimed came from playing the drums. Arlo was an accomplished musician; he had played on the albums of some very well known rock stars, but his own band had failed to cut a single album. He got headaches trying to figure out what they were doing wrong. The truth is, the other members of the band were not nearly the musicians that Arlo was. However, I found his loyalty to them endearing. I sometimes thought I could fall in love with Arlo, but then he would do something like talk too much about the celebrities at his sister's club, or throw a beer can out of his window and I could not help but compare him to George. George did not litter and he was not impressed with fame. In fact, he had little curiosity about others' lives. He never read gossip columns, nor did he ask questions about a neighbor's divorce or an eerie tale of child abuse. If we passed a burning building or a car accident, he did not stop amid the other gapers to watch.

"It's you I'm interested in," George always told me.

Arlo put his arms around me and I could smell the slight aroma of shampoo. When I felt his hair, it was still damp.

"I missed you," Arlo said. "You don't visit me enough." There was a bit of a whine in his voice but I ignored it.

"I try," I said.

Arlo kissed me and I thought of telling him right then about my newly acquired inheritance. If Arlo had more money he might leave his band for good and strike out on his own, finally make a career as a drummer. I thought of giving my money to him. Then I kissed him again and the thought passed.

Arlo and I enjoyed making love to each other, even when his sister was in the room. Arlo's bed was built above the rest of the apartment on stilts and when we were up there we pretended we were king and queen surveying our domain. We discussed Irene's future at the club, we moved furniture around in our minds, we placed orders from the kitchen, and sometimes Arlo stared at his drums in the corner and practiced a difficult set on them for me in his mind. Then we made love as if our subjects were there watching, learning from us how it should be done. We were passionate and talkative. Arlo sometimes narrated our actions and it made me laugh.

"Now I will use my tongue to send shivers down her spine," Arlo said. And when he did, I shivered.

"Now I will kiss the most beautiful girl in the world," Arlo said. "First her lips, then her lovely neck. Then her right breast. Look at that perfect chin, those earlobes." I blushed.

"Now he prepares for penetration," Arlo said. He held me tighter until I nearly cried.

As we finished, Arlo said, "Now he closes his eyes and imagines she will never leave him." Arlo closed his eyes.

But of course we both knew I would leave him soon. It was after five and George, although not a suspicious man, would wonder why I was not at home.

Just before leaving Arlo's place, I told him about Uncle Theodore's money.

"Holy shit," Arlo said, and Irene turned over and moaned from her bed. "That's amazing," Arlo said, this time a bit more quietly.

"I know," I said.

"What are you going to do with the money?" he said.

"I'm going to have a big Thanksgiving dinner," I said, but I knew, as with George, that was not what Arlo meant.

"But what else?" Arlo said.

"I haven't decided yet," I said.

"If you need help deciding," Arlo said. "I'm your man."

"I'll keep that in mind," I said.

"Don't forget me in your will," Arlo said. Then he kissed me as if he were kissing one of the celebrities at Irene's club, his eyes peering over my shoulder to see if anyone was watching. "Truly amazing," Arlo said.

"Isn't it, though," I said, and then I said good-bye.

I wondered as I walked up the darkening city streets toward home why I remained unfaithful to George. I was not particularly unhappy with him, nor did I regret our marriage. I even believed in monogamy. I believed what I was doing was wrong. When I came home to George after being with Arlo, I tried to do little things to assuage my guilt. I cleaned the house or baked cinnamon bread, which George loved. I would even look through the newspaper ads with him for larger apartments and houses for sale, as if I believed we really would move, have a baby. Sometimes I even wanted to tell George where I had been, much as a criminal sometimes feels a need for a confession.

"Don't you know," I felt like shouting to George, "I've been with another man?" But George suspected nothing. He never asked me where I went when I was out.

Sometimes I thought I even did it because George made it so easy. There was no sneaking behind his back; no lies to rearrange and plot; if I met a man, I did not even need to tell him I was married. I did not tell Arlo the first time we were together, and the second time we met, when I finally told him about my husband, he was surprised.

"You don't seem married at all," Arlo said.

"I guess that's why I'm here with you," I said to him. "I don't seem married to me, either."

Of course, there was something unnerving about all of this trust. As if, like me, George had his own secrets that he did not need to work hard to keep. And perhaps, like George, I just wasn't looking for what I did not want to see.

When George came home that night he was carrying a large bouquet of flowers. There were yellow daffodils and white daisies. The card attached read: "For the woman who holds my future in her heart."

"That's lovely," I said. "So poetic." I smelled the flowers' sweet smell and sighed.

"It's true," said George.

I took our vase down off the top of the refrigerator where it was stored and filled it with water. Then I placed each stem in one by one, first a daffodil, then a daisy. The result was nothing like the elaborate flower arrangements one sees at the florist.

"Do you understand the card?" George asked. He was sitting on the bed watching me work with the flowers. He had kicked off his shoes and they had fallen one on top of the other, protectively almost. George did not wait for me to answer. "It means it's time," he said.

"Time for what?" I asked. I did not look at him, but fussed with my flowers. I pushed some stems down, others up. Then I moved the vase three times on the table.

"We can afford it now," George continued. "We can afford a litter of them."

"George," I said.

He had come up behind me and slipped his arms around my waist. He kissed my neck, familiar and warm, and I thought how different George's kiss was from Arlo's. Of course, I had known George for a very long time. Ever since that party during my senior year when George had made promises a man doesn't usually make when he first meets a girl.

"I don't need to know you better," he had told me then. "Because I know what I want so well."

In the years before, with the others I had dated, I was always caring for them—driving the car when they did too many drugs, making pots of coffee during exams, treating them kindly in bed—and then, when their needs were not so strong, no longer so compelling, always leaving. But George had seemed older than these boys, he seemed someone who would watch over me as I grew, someone who would make sure I grew up right.

"That's all you two will do is grow up," Walter had said after I introduced him to George for the first time.

"What do you mean?" I said.

"He just seems so old, Annie," Walter said. "I don't want it to happen to you."

"But I do," I said, and I moved into George's small off-campus apartment within the month.

George kissed me again, and whispered something in my ear. It was either "lady" or "a baby."

"I'm not ready," I said pulling away, but he held me tight in his strong arms.

"Listen to me, Anne," George said, and he would not let me go. "I've always wanted children. Even when I was a child. I wanted to give my kids a life I never had."

"That's not a good reason," I said, still struggling.

"Please," George said, his breath heavy on my neck.

"Let me go," I said.

"Anne," George said. He pushed his lips against mine and squeezed my body so hard I could barely breathe.

"Stop it," I said, and when he didn't I kicked him as if he were a mugger trying to grab my purse or the strand of pearls from around my neck. I kicked him the way I had been taught in the class I took at the gym, as hard as I could with the heel of my shoe against his shins. I still do not know why I did it; it was not out of self-defense. I knew he was not really a criminal, but rather George my husband, who was only trying to make me change my mind.

George immediately dropped his arms and moaned. His face twisted in pain and he limped over to the bed and fell down with a thump.

"It wasn't that hard," I hoped.

George would not look at me, and when he pulled the leg of his pants up above his knee, I could see the red imprint of my heel, already like a scar or an ugly birthmark that would not fade away.

George went to bed early without dinner and I sat up alone. First I watched television, then I read at the table, my back straight and unyielding in the small wooden chair. At eight o'clock the telephone rang, but the person on the other end hung up. At nine it rang again. This time it was Arlo.

"Anne," he said. He was whispering, though of course there was no need for that on his side of the line. "I missed you."

Arlo had never called me at home before and I did not at first recognize his voice. I said nothing for a long time, but glanced over to where George slept soundly, his large body sprawled diagonally across our bed. Then I thought about what I would say, but all I could think of was, "Hello, hello, hello."

"Come visit me," Arlo said. "I miss you."

"Hello," I said again.

"Anne," Arlo said. "Come now. I miss you."

Then I hung up.

I could not concentrate on my book, but sat in the dim light and thought about Arlo and the phone call, and then about George. I felt sorry for kicking him, felt somewhat like those abusive parents one reads about in the newspaper—they cannot control the violence they use against those they love. I even thought about babies. First, just the images of babies I had from television and magazine ads. Then about the baby George and I might have —the color of its hair, the shape of its face. Then I remembered a conversation my father and I had about me when I was a baby. There were few photographs of me in the family album, and I had asked him why.

"The most frustrating time in my life was when you were an infant," my father answered me. "I had been looking forward to your arrival for so long, and then there you were in your crib, helpless, crying. When I asked you what was wrong you only cried more."

"Annie has always been rotten," Walter had said, grinning from across the room.

"You were a difficult baby," my father said to me.

I looked down at the album in my lap, at the two small photographs of myself as an infant. My hair was even lighter then, and a small curl stuck to my forehead. I was lying on a couch, wrapped in a blanket, not held by anyone. My eyes were squinting at the light of the flashbulb, my mouth closed in a tight pinch.

"But you were happy, weren't you?" I had asked my father.

He paused. "Of course I was happy to have you," he

said. "But it made me old quick. Unfortunately your mother felt the same way."

"Mom felt that way all the time," Walter said.

"True enough," my father said. Then he and Walter had started talking about something else.

I remembered closing the family photograph album, going into my bedroom, and crying for the longest time. To this day I do not understand why.

At ten-thirty, Arlo called the apartment again and I answered it on the first ring.

"Where are you?" he said.

"Here," I answered.

"I wish you were here," Arlo said. It was a strange tone of voice, one I was not familiar with. It sounded as if he was trying to persuade me of something—of his devotion to me, of his sincerity?

"I can't talk," I whispered. I could hear George breathing heavily; he had again slept through the ringing of the phone.

"I know," Arlo said. Then, after a pause, "I've fallen in love with you." It was not I love you, but I've fallen in love, as if love were something happening to him that he had no control over.

"I don't think so," I said.

"I want to see you," Arlo said.

"I've got to go," I said, and I hung up again.

I do not pretend to know the human heart. It seems to me a strange, capricious organ, easily bruised but rarely suffering terminal injury. In our temporary arrangement, I had always assumed Arlo's heart had not even been touched. Perhaps I was mistaken, for that was not the last I was to hear of him that week or even that night. He called me three more times, at eleven, at one, and then at three. At one point George did wake up, and when I said it was a prank caller he told me, uncannily, to stop being so nice to strangers. Always too nice. Then he fell back asleep. Arlo kept calling me, though, that week at work and in the evenings when I returned. He told me he loved me as if it was something he needed me to believe, as if it would change something between us, though of course it would not. I did not know why he called so often, and so suddenly. Arlo, despite his affection for me, had always kept his distance from my home and private life. He did not seem to want to know much about me, and there was comfort in that. Now it got so I feared answering the telephone, and although I had originally planned on spending another afternoon with Arlo, I found myself making excuses as to why I could not.

It was true there was much to be done before the Thanksgiving feast. Although it would only be the four of us—George and me, Walter and Allegra—I did not intend to leave anything out, and I shopped all week for fresh fruits and vegetables, ordering my turkey at a poultry shop and raw oysters at the fish market. I polished the silver and cleaned the crystal George and I had received as wedding gifts and had never used. On the Wednesday before Thanksgiving, I even ordered a large arrangement of cut flowers for the center of the table. I was pleased with my efforts, and all Wednesday night I kept opening and closing the refrigerator just to gaze at all the food, making certain each time that nothing had been forgotten.

At seven-thirty that night Arlo called again. I was elbow deep in flour, making dough for the pies I would fill in the morning. The first batch of dough had already shredded into tiny pieces and had to be thrown away. The second batch was not faring much better and I patched it like a quilt until it fit into the pie tin. George was out buying candles, which I had somehow forgotten, and I let the telephone ring many times before I answered it.

"Hello," I finally shouted into the receiver.

"It's me," Arlo said.

Of course it is, I felt like saying, but did not. Instead I said, "You've got to stop calling me at home."

"I have a reason," Arlo said. "I want you to come hear my band play tonight."

"Arlo," I said.

"It's a club near where you live," Arlo continued.

"I'm sorry," I said. "I'm getting ready for Thanksgiving." I balanced the phone between my neck and chin and pressed the edges of the dough down against the pie tin with a fork.

"Oh, that's right," Arlo said.

"I'm covered with flour and dough right now," I said.

"Dough?" said Arlo, laughing. "What are you doing? Playing with your inheritance?" There was a nasty edge to his humor.

"What are you talking about?" I said.

"Just teasing," Arlo said. Then, quite seriously, "Don't let this money change you. Don't let it come between us."

"Don't be stupid," I said.

Arlo tried once more, this time his voice was softer, kinder. "Come tonight, Anne," he said. "I really need you there."

And, although I found it difficult, I said again I was sorry. I couldn't possibly go, not tonight. Then, as I hung up the phone, it hit me. Unexpectedly, yet also irrevocably, that it was the inheritance. That was the reason behind the sudden rash of phone calls from Arlo, the seriousness with which he was suddenly taking his feelings for me. It had nothing to do with love, but was somehow connected to Uncle Theodore's money.

Later, when I told Walter the story of Arlo and the money, he did not believe me.

"You're looney," Walter said. "It wasn't the money. It was you. He loved you."

"We weren't that serious," I said.

"You wish," Walter said.

"He loved the money," I said. "And it wasn't even that much."

"If you insist," said Walter.

At any rate, I decided I would not see Arlo again. I did feel sad, then I was relieved. It was almost as if I had planned it to happen, made up the story about the inheritance, anticipated Arlo's needs, his reaction. He could not help himself, and I decided I would send Arlo something when the money arrived to help him with his music. And I would include a gift for Irene as well.

Placing my hands on my knees, I peered once more into the well-stocked refrigerator and smiled. Then I wrapped my finished pie crusts with Saran and placed them into the refrigerator with the other food. I felt suddenly very charitable and kind; I couldn't possibly be the same person who had kicked my husband in the leg, who had actually cheated on him behind his back. And when George returned home with the candles, I kissed him and told him again and again that I was sorry, very, very, sorry.

It was raining Thanksgiving morning, a loud rain that angrily hit the windows of the small apartment like blows to the head. I had been up early struggling with the turkey, a pale damp bird that looked nothing like something people might eat. The dishes my mother had created so effortlessly required a skill in the kitchen I did not possess. First my stuffing was too dry, then too wet. The squash tasted bitter. George helped me with the cranberry sauce and the yams and they at least were a semblance of my mother's dishes from the past. The oysters, fortunately, would be eaten raw and only required fresh lemon.

In the afternoon I set the table and dressed. I had bought a new outfit for the occasion—a dark blue velvet dress that made me feel a bit like a china doll, fragile and lovely. It matched my eyes. Even the rain subsided and George opened the windows to let in the brisk November air.

Just before Walter and Allegra's arrival, George turned to me. "You look pretty," he said.

I smiled. "This is going to be a perfect Thanksgiving," I said. And I forgot about my father, who would not be coming, about the lopsided pies in the oven, forgot about Arlo even, and really believed the Thanksgiving would be exactly what I wanted.

When Walter and I were children we used to play a game we called "Worst Case." It was an easy game to play, requiring no board, dice, or cards. First Walter would place me in a terrible predicament, a worst-case scenario—"You're getting on the Lexington Avenue subway line and all your clothes disappear," or "Dad and I die in a car accident and you're left alone and alive in the backseat"—and I would have to tell Walter how I would react, what I would do. Then it was my turn to place Walter in a similar nightmare, and he would be required to answer back to me. We played the game more frequently than some would consider healthy, but it never failed to make us feel brave, as if we had actually lived through the imagined situations—and even more,

96

it made our own life seem quite easy, almost happy in comparison.

I still play the game today, though of course not with Walter. I present worst cases for myself all the time; that way I am never disappointed, never unprepared for what often does occur. However, I forgot to do it for Thanksgiving, and when Walter and Allegra arrived at the apartment I felt a bit too happy, too at ease.

"Walter has told me all about you," Allegra said. She was a short, pretty girl, but something like a puppy as well. She trotted about the apartment, even knocked over a chair at one point, and she seemed to sidle up against Walter as if she were trying to climb up his leg. "Of course, Walter never told me how beautiful you were," and Allegra beamed at me, showing all her teeth.

"I don't like to brag," Walter said.

"Oh really," I said.

We sat down to dinner and George poured the champagne. I brought out the oysters.

"You don't eat these, do you?" Allegra said. She picked up one of the oysters between her thumb and index finger and held it out as if it were moldy cheese or spoiled fish.

"Some of us do," George said.

"Not this lady," Allegra said.

Walter ignored her and finished his glass of champagne in one quick gulp. Pouring himself another glass, he offered up a toast.

"To Annie," he said, standing up before us. "May she never do without anything or anyone." Walter grinned as big as could be, and, clinking his glass against mine, he downed the champagne.

"With her fortune she won't have to," said Allegra.

97

George frowned and swallowed an oyster whole. He did not touch his glass.

"We used to have a prayer when we were young," I said, but no one paid me any mind.

"Pass the bottle," Walter said.

"Oh yes," Allegra said.

Just then, as if on cue, there was a flutter of gray feathers in the air above the table. Allegra screamed and dropped her glass of champagne on the floor, where I watched our good crystal shatter into pieces.

"It's a flying rat," Allegra cried out.

"I think it's a pigeon," George said.

We discovered it was a sparrow come in from the chilly November air. Disoriented and frightened, it circled our dinner table once more, then landed on top of the refrigerator in a heap.

Everyone but Allegra rose from the table to corner the refrigerator. We stared at the bird as it stared back, its small dark eyes like glass, only softer.

"What should we do?" I said.

"Broil it with the turkey," Walter suggested.

"We'll have to catch it," George said very seriously. "A wild bird in the house means terrible bad luck."

"I've heard that," Allegra said.

"I always thought it meant you were going to have six more weeks of winter," said Walter.

"That's the groundhog," said Allegra, and she giggled through her nose.

"My mistake," said Walter.

"It's not funny," George said. I thought he might even cry. "This is sure to bring bad news, most likely death." George took my hand and squeezed it hard. The sparrow on top of the refrigerator sat like a carved decoy.

"I'll catch it," Walter said.

"Don't kill it," I said.

Thanksgiving dinner was completely forgotten while Walter and George struggled to catch the bird with a broom and grocery bag. They ran about the small apartment swatting at the air with the broom, looking not so much like hunters but like the hunted, caught in a trap. The sparrow was quick and small and would not be caught. Allegra, bored already, watched television from George's and my bed. I stirred the yams, poked at the turkey, watched everything overcook, dry out.

It was quite late when they finally caught the bird and set it free outside the window. Walter had finished off the first bottle of champagne and then another. George muttered about bad luck, death. At last they trapped the sparrow in a corner, George swept it gently into the bag, Walter snapped it shut.

"Out with the bad luck," Walter said, closing the window behind the swish of the sparrow's wings.

"I wish it was that easy," George said.

Allegra had fallen asleep on the bed, her shoes half off her feet, her long hair in a tangle.

"I guess I better take the lady home," Walter said, looking at Allegra with something between affection and curiosity.

"I guess you better," said George.

"But what about dinner?" I said.

Walter pulled me close and hugged me. "I'm sorry, Annie," he whispered in my ear. "It looks like it's time to call it a night."

"It does to me," George said.

"But what about all the food I cooked?" I said. "What about Thanksgiving dinner?"

Walter shrugged. "I'm not very hungry anymore," he

said. Then, shaking Allegra awake, the two of them stumbled out the door.

"Thank you so much," Allegra called out. "It was nice meeting you."

"Take it easy, Annie," Walter said.

"Oh sure," I said.

There was nothing to cry about. George and I ate some of the turkey and stuffing and I threw out the yams and bottled the cranberry sauce for another night. Neither of us spoke much. I was thinking of my failed Thanksgiving. George was thinking about the bird in the house.

"I hope no one dies," he said at one point.

"I hope so too," I said.

After we finished eating, George helped me clean up the dishes. I washed the china and crystal, he dried.

"This happened twice before," George said as he placed the fluted champagne glasses on the shelf. "When I was a child." He paused for a moment as if for strength, then continued. "The first time we found a wild bird in the house my grandmother was hit by a car and died the next day. The second time, my father beat my sister up and she ran away to California."

"But she didn't die," I said.

"It was the same," George said. He dried the same plate over and over again. I continued to wash the dishes. The apartment seemed empty and sad.

Suddenly I knew what had to be done, something pure and right.

"We need a Thanksgiving prayer," I said, and, leaving the rest of the dishes in the sink, I swung George around.

"What?" he said.

"We always had a Thanksgiving blessing," I said. "Maybe tonight it will keep the bad luck away."

George did not look very hopeful, but he followed as I led him to the table.

I relit the candles, and we stood next to each other around the table, our shoulders touching. I bowed my head and George did the same.

"We thank God for all that he has given us," I started, and my voice sounded not quite like mine. "For our health and our happy times, and our good fortune." Then, very softly although still strong, I said, "And for our family."

George leaned his head against mine and his familiar smell was comforting and reassuring. He was here with me this Thanksgiving and if we could avoid the bad luck of the sparrow we would be together next year as well.

"And for *our* family," I said again, and this time I knew what I meant and I think George did, too. He echoed with me a loud and joyous amen.

BAD NEIGHBORS

Despite the advice of my father, I bought the house for cash.

"You've got to make your money work for you," my father said. And later, "Don't be silly, Annie, everyone has a mortgage."

But I had the money from my inheritance and it seemed tedious to go through a bank. Besides, I did not want to think about the purchase every month; problems are bound to appear in homes, particularly older ones, and paying a mortgage the day the plumbing fails or the evening you find a small leak in the roof would be too much to bear.

The house was located in a small town in Connecticut, almost an hour and a half from the city, but only a few minutes from the train that George took every morning to work.

It was not a particularly large house, but compared to
our small apartment in the city I felt as if I were living in a
cavernous castle. I even came to call it that: My Castle.
There were three bedrooms off the main hall stairs and
another smaller bedroom and bath off a narrow back
stairway leading from the kitchen. George told me that
this small room must have first been meant for a maid.
Downstairs the living room and dining room were airy,
with windows on three sides, and the old wooden floor
creaked whenever you walked. The kitchen was exactly
the size of our entire old apartment; George squared it off
with a tape measure. There were hooks on the ceiling on
which to attach pots and pans, and blue and white ce-
ramic tiles above the stove and around the sink. There
was even an old stone fireplace which we had been
advised did indeed work, although the previous owner
had kept it filled with a large kettle of dried flowers.

It was the first house we looked at, and although the
real estate agent suggested we might want something more
convenient to the city, or closer to couples our own age,
we felt awed by the prospect of looking at more houses,
of making any more decisions. Even George, who is always so practical, said, "Buy it," with a spontaneity un-
like anything I had ever seen in him before.

The first week in the house was uneventful. George
took a few days off from work to help unpack our few
boxes of belongings and we spent long hours waiting for
various servicemen to show up—to hook up our phones,
turn on our water and electricity, install the refrigerator.

At one point, right after the telephone had been
hooked up, I said to George, "I feel like this is all happening to someone else." Then I picked up the new white
receiver and listened for a moment to the dial tone, half

expecting someone to speak, call me by a new name, give me my identity.

"No, it's really happening to us," George said. He seemed delighted with the move. He stared out the back windows at our large stretch of lawn, thoroughly relieved that finally he owned something in the world. George relished the idea of cutting the lawn, of weeding the small beds of flowers near the house, of raking large piles of damp leaves in the fall. He hungered to put a fresh coat of paint in the small bedroom, to wallpaper the bathrooms. George had been born and raised in a house; these chores did not seem insurmountable to him.

"I feel like the lady who lived here before," I said, and placed the receiver down with a click. Since Arlo, I had been faithful to George, had not even been tempted to stray. I told myself I had finally outgrown that need, and although I was rightly proud, I also worried that I was giving up something dear and important, as well.

"We didn't really know the last owner," George said. There was a puzzled look on his usually serene face. "And she was near her seventies, at least."

I shrugged. "Perhaps not exactly like her," I said, remembering the widow in her dowdy flowered dress, her high scratchy voice. "But certainly not like me, either."

"You sure look like you," George said, kissing my neck with surprising tenderness.

"Do I?" I said, and I touched my face with the tips of my fingers, as if I were blind and trying to make sure the face was mine.

The second week in the new house, George returned to work and I was left alone in my castle for the first time. Although there was much to be done, I found each of the tasks overwhelming. This was nothing like my job at the bookstore in the city, where tasks were broken down into

104

neat categories—stocking, selling, cataloging—with distinct times allotted for each one. Here the day loomed long ahead of me; the vacuuming and dusting alone could easily have occupied the entire morning.

Instead of tackling even this one chore, I walked outside to the backyard. It was late spring and bees hovered overhead and the air was thick with the scent of flowers. Our own backyard was sorely in need of work—the grass wanted mowing, bushes and shrubs invaded upon each other, tangling together in a mass of thorns and greens. A branch from one of our trees swung dangerously close to our neighbor's house. I would have to tell George, and then what would he do? Would he climb the tree himself, wielding a large axe and a power saw? I imagined him up there in the tree, swinging high above the ground, peering into our neighbor's window.

"Don't worry," George would say. "I can cut trees. I can cut an entire forest."

It was then that I first noticed our neighbor.

He was out in his own garden wearing a yellow golfing hat and a pair of khaki shorts that reached down to his knees. His legs looked white and thin and he was carrying a trowel and a circle of rope. I could not see his face—he was bent over examining something in the soil—but I placed him in his fifties, perhaps even older, since he was home on a weekday the other men, certainly younger men, would be at work. I thought of waving hello—it seemed a proper neighborly gesture—but he seemed so intent on whatever he was looking at that I did not want to interrupt. It turned out, however, that it was he who recognized me first. After peering down at the ground for what seemed like quite a few minutes, he began to stand up slowly, almost one inch at a time. When he was finally upright, he gazed toward my new house and then at me. It took a moment for his eyes to focus, or perhaps just to register my presence.

He finally shouted hello across the lawn, waving the trowel in the air. "Welcome, neighbor."

We met each other halfway, where our two properties met. Upon closer examination he was not as old as I had first imagined, or perhaps he just had a younger-looking face. At any rate, he looked harmless, the kind of man one expected to meet in a Connecticut suburb. His real name was Nathaniel Hartley, he told me, but everyone called him Hart. He asked if I would mind calling him Hart as well.

I had expected us to merely introduce ourselves and then go on our ways, however I discovered my new neighbor liked to talk. He sat cross-legged on the grass, placed his trowel and rope beside him, and motioned for me to sit down as well.

"Nature's chair," he remarked pleasantly, as I shifted uncomfortably on the grass; I was not in the habit of paying social visits in my backyard. Then Hart began to tell me about himself.

Although only in his early fifties, I discovered he was retired.

"I didn't work for it," he admitted as if this were a source of contention. "I was given it all," and he waved at the house, at the backyard, even at his own clothing, as if the yellow hat and khaki shorts were also part of his inheritance.

He told me he had lived in this house for nearly twenty years and his pride and joy was his garden. It was indeed a beautiful garden. Flowers of assorted variety and color were arranged in well-defined rows and the shrubs were neatly trimmed. There was even a small vegetable plot in the far back right. I could see the white stakes bearing the name of the fruit or vegetable that would soon rise from that particular spot.

I was surprised to learn Hart was not married, or more accurately that his wife had left him many years before and that he had one son who was fifteen.

"I've raised Henry myself," Hart told me. Then, looking down at his shoes, which were old worn moccasins, he sighed. "Lately Henry and I have not been getting along well."

"I'm sorry to hear that," I said, and I thought of my own father raising Walter and me. Then I remembered the year my mother first left, not like a death, but worse, and I really did feel sorry for poor Hart, and for his son, Henry, whom I had not even met.

"He has taken on some very bad habits," Hart continued.

"Teenagers are usually rebellious," I said, trying to be helpful. I tried to imagine what a man like Hart might consider a bad habit—did Henry bite his nails, chew with his mouth open, walk through the house barefoot? Or perhaps it really was more serious. Perhaps the boy was a thief, or a drug addict. I imagined Henry sitting on the back steps late at night throwing empty bottles of Jim Crow into our backyard.

"It's that neighbor's son again," George would say. "He really should get some help."

"It's a terribly bad habit," I might reply. "Throwing empty bottles into our backyard."

Hart stuck an index finger into the soil as if to check for depth. "It's not mere rebellion," he said. Then he picked up a long blade of grass and slid it up and down his pale leg. I looked down at the ground, then back toward my house, anywhere but at this strange talkative man. "It's not just the bizarre clothing and music; I expected that. It's become far more serious. It's beyond my control.''

Hart looked about to cry and I thought of making up an excuse, telling him I had to go inside to make a phone call, to take my wash out of the dryer, but before I could say a word, he unexpectedly touched the top of my shoulders with both his hands, as if he were going to pull me forward into an embrace. Startled, I jumped, upsetting both of us in our rather precarious positions in the grass. Hart nearly toppled over.

''I didn't mean to frighten you,'' he said, although of course that is exactly what he had done. ''I just feel I can talk to you.'' He righted himself once more, crossing his legs, putting out his hands for balance.

''I don't think so,'' I said, rising to my feet. ''You don't even know me.''

''But you're my neighbor,'' he said, as if I were his sister or a close aunt. ''And you have a much more compassionate face than my last neighbor.''

''Mrs. Beasley,'' I said. That was the woman I had bought the house from.

''Mrs. Beasley was very uncompassionate,'' Hart said.

''I think you will find me the same way,'' I said. Then, indeed making up some excuse about a phone call, I darted back to my house. I waved to him just before I entered my back door. He was still sitting in the grass, looking even closer to tears than before. I hoped he would get up soon and go back inside his own house, or go back to work on his garden. I thought it might do us both some good.

The day following my talk with Hart I really did stay inside the house and work. I not only vacuumed and dusted, but lined all the shelves in the kitchen with white

shelf paper, scrubbed the tiles in each of the three bathrooms, and washed all the windows from the inside. The
day after that it rained and I did not go out, and the next
day I left the house early to go into town and do some
shopping. There were only three stores in the entire town—a
grocery store, a hardware store, and a gift shop. I found
nothing in them to interest me, but wandered through
them for hours just the same.

I saw very little of George that week. He was working
late at the office and his commute to and from the city on
the train added even more hours to our time apart. When
George did finally get home, he was fretful and tired. He
ate his dinner in a hurry without speaking and then went
just as quickly to bed and to sleep. He did not wait for me
to join him, he barely kissed me good night. I believe I
understood why. We had been trying for the last few
months to have a baby, but were so far unsuccessful;
George's sperm count was too low. George had believed
that the move to Connecticut might help, but now, not
even through our second week in the new house, he
seemed to have given up on even trying.

"Why bother," George said. "Why bother with anything at all," and he very deliberately bumped his head
three times against our new bedroom door.

When I told my brother Walter about the problem,
he laughed, "Are you sure you're doing it right, Annie?"
he said.

"It's not funny," I said.

"I'm sorry," Walter said. "But I just think you've got
to give it more time."

"It's been since Thanksgiving," I said.

"What's a few months when you're having fun," said
Walter.

"Oh sure," I said.

* * *

It was not until Friday that I again saw Hart. He was working in the far back of his yard, in the vegetable garden, and he was wearing the same yellow hat and khaki shorts. He was digging; he would dig for a time and then wipe his neck with a white handkerchief he kept in his back pocket. I watched him for a while and was just about to go back inside when I heard the back door of Hart's house slam shut and a boy, who I was certain was Henry, walked out into the sunshine.

He was not dressed as strangely as his father had led me to believe, certainly no differently than the hundreds of teenagers I saw in the streets of New York. Although it was hot, the boy wore long jeans and a large black leather belt with metal studs. His purple T-shirt was emblazoned with silver stars, and on his wrists he wore miniature versions of his black belt. His hair was cut in a crewcut and was dyed a bright unnatural orange. I could not see if he was wearing an earring, though something did glimmer near the left side of his neck. He walked, not as if in a hurry, but in a quick, somewhat confused pace. When he reached his father, Hart stopped digging, leaned on the shovel, and looked up at his son, who was almost three inches taller. They said something to each other, I could not hear what. At one point, Hart threw down the shovel in disgust. Henry pulled his fingers through his orange hair. I imagined some sort of disagreement and wondered what it was about this time. What had Henry done?

Although I have been taught by my father not to interfere in other people's lives, to stay within the insular and consuming knowledge of my own family, I could not help myself. I walked out toward the edge of our two properties and called hello. Both Hart and Henry looked up.

"It's Anne," Hart shouted as if not so much greeting me, but announcing my presence to the world and to Henry. "How are you, dear?" Hart asked.

I saw Hart take Henry's arm and walk him out to meet me. We gathered in the spot where Hart and I had sat talking a few days earlier.

"This is our lovely new neighbor Anne," Hart told his son.

Henry nodded.

"Wonderful day, isn't it?" Hart said. "Everything is so green after the rain."

I agreed, and thought for a moment that Hart was going to disappoint me, that I was not to learn about Henry after all, but that was not to be the case.

Using his handkerchief, Hart wiped some perspiration from his brow, then sighed. "Henry and I were just having a disagreement," Hart said finally. "Perhaps you could be an impartial judge."

"I don't know," I said. I looked to Henry to see his reaction, but there was no expression on his face, just a blank look as if he had taken a fair number of Valium or Quaaludes, or perhaps was just in a very deep daydream.

"Henry believes there should be no laws governing man," Hart said. "Isn't that right, Henry?" Henry gave no sign of acknowledgment.

Hart continued. "Henry stole my car last night, drove it into New York, and left it there."

I looked toward Hart's driveway; there was no car parked there. I could not remember if I had noticed a car there on previous days. "How did you get home from the city?" I asked Henry.

Henry shrugged.

111

"He took the train," Hart said. "He simply couldn't remember where he had parked the car. Couldn't remember," Hart repeated.

"I'll find the car," Henry said. His voice was high-pitched, yet soft. "It's somewhere."

"Somewhere!" Hart said. He was growing more and more agitated; his face was red and damp and he wiped it again with his handkerchief.

"I only borrowed it," Henry said.

"You stole it," Hart said. Then, looking at me, "What do you think, Anne? Don't you think he stole it?"

I did not know what to say and stood there, looking from Henry to Hart and then back to Henry again, waiting for some kind of clue. I wasn't certain that it would actually be called stealing, since the car belonged to the boy's father. I wondered what George would say, and I thought of dashing into the house and calling him at work. But how would I explain myself? That I had been called upon to judge a fight between a father and son I didn't even know? Was there a precedent case in the law books that George might quote?

"Of course he stole the car," Hart said. "You're just too well mannered to say so."

"I'm sure he'll find it," I said.

Henry looked at me in such a way that I almost felt sorry for the boy. After all, it couldn't be easy living with a father like that. Then it dawned on me; Hart had told me his son was fifteen, and fifteen was too young to drive a car in Connecticut or New York. He couldn't have a driver's license, not even a learner's permit. This was an issue I could deal with.

"Aren't you too young to be driving a car?" I asked Henry. "You're only fifteen."

"Why don't you mind your own fucking business," Henry said. "Before something bad happens to you."

I flushed, and Hart winced like a man with a severe cramp in his side.

Then Henry winked at me, a lewd wink, and grinned. "Just kidding," he said. "You can bother me anytime you want." Then, assuming that same blank look on his face, Henry strode quickly back to his house, slamming the door behind him.

Hart apologized again and again. "I told you he was difficult," Hart said. "I warned you."

"Don't worry about it," I said. "I'm sure it's just a phase." Then, feeling suddenly chilled, although it must have been in the mid-eighties outside, I told Hart good-bye and hurried back into my own house. I even locked the door.

That night at dinner, late after George's train had arrived, I told him the story.

"Just what we need," George said. "Bad neighbors." Then, pouring himself a glass of wine, he said, "If I were you Anne, I'd stay clear of them."

"But he's always out there working in his garden," I said. I had made a cold pasta dish for dinner and had bought a crunchy loaf of French bread, but I was too agitated to eat. I swirled the pasta around on my plate, letting the oil separate, the noodles dry. I kept seeing Henry, with his orange hair, wearing his purple T-shirt, and wandering the streets of New York late at night, searching for the lost car.

"I know I put it somewhere," Henry kept saying in his high voice. "How easily cars disappear nowadays." And he looked small and scared and all alone.

"I can't stay inside the house all day," I said to George. "And I'm sure Hart is just lonely. Henry too."

"Hart?" George said. "You call him Hart."

"That's what everyone calls him," I said.

George mopped up the sauce on his plate with a piece of bread and said nothing for what seemed a very long time. Then, looking at me, he said, "Anne, I wouldn't get involved with people like that. Obviously there are a lot of problems in the family. You don't want the boy borrowing our car some night, now, do you?"

With the small amount of money remaining from my inheritance, George and I had bought a used car. It was a '75 Toyota painted blue, with a manual transmission that stuck sometimes in reverse. It was the first car I had ever owned and I sat in it sometimes, even when I had no place to go. George had taught me how to drive the car with little patience for the numerous times I stalled at red lights and inclines on the roadway. I still did not feel comfortable driving and there was a good amount of fear involved every time I turned the ignition key on.

"I don't think Henry is a real car thief," I said.

"No, he's worse," George said. "He's a boy looking for trouble."

"I'm sure that's not true," I said. I do not know why I was defending Hart and his son; that afternoon they had certainly startled me. But somehow with George, I had taken a proprietary air about our neighbors. *I* knew them; George did not. "I'm sure they're both just very unhappy," I said to George.

"Since when did you become so compassionate?" George said.

The word sounded familiar. Then I remembered that was what Hart had told me he had been looking for that first day out in the garden—compassion. "What do you take me for?" I said. "A Mrs. Beasley?"

George looked at me, confused. Pushing his empty

114

plate away, he shook his head. "I don't understand you at all, Anne," he said. Then, his voice patient and strained, "Why don't you get involved in some activity? Why don't you get away from the house for the day? Why don't you do something?"

He did not say so, but I was certain he was thinking of the baby I had not yet produced. Why didn't I do that, he might as easily have said, as if it *were* something I could do, like shopping or reading a book.

"I don't understand you," George repeated, and with one wave of his arm across the table, he swept all the dishes clattering to the floor.

Although startled, I only shrugged, then knelt beside the table to clean up the mess.

When the phone rang late that night I was certain it would be my father. He called often since the move, and at odd times during the day and night. He always sounded somewhat nervous over the phone—he asked me again and again what I had eaten for breakfast or dinner, and whether the house was still standing, still watertight, and he questioned me on the weather.

"Is it raining there?" he might ask. "Are the skies very threatening?"

"We have the same weather in Connecticut as you have in New York," I would tell him. "It's hot and sunny."

"But Annie," my father would then reply. "Are you eating well?"

It was as if by my move out of the city, away from my father's realm, I had rendered myself available to all the dangers in the world. Tornadoes, floods, even famine, were lurking right outside my Connecticut door. George was helpless to protect me, I was helpless to protect myself.

When I answered the phone that night, however, it

was not my father, but instead a strange male voice that sounded somehow familiar. It was Henry, my neighbor's son.

"Anne," he said. "It's me."

"Hello?" I said.

"You've got to help me," Henry said. His high voice grew stronger. "I'm in trouble," he said.

"It's very late," I said, and then, "Shouldn't you talk to your father?"

"Who is it?" George asked from our bed, but he was reading a book and did not expect a reply.

"I can't talk to my father," Henry said, and then, "I thought you could help me. You have a kind face."

I had never thought of myself as having a kind face. It was a thin angular face. I had once, long ago, been approached to do some modeling for a teen magazine, but my father had refused to sign the release form.

"You don't need outsiders telling you how pretty you are," my father said to me when he found me crying in my room. "We all know you're pretty."

He had said nothing about me looking kind, however. No one ever had.

"I don't think I can help you," I said to Henry.

"Just listen," he said. Then Henry began talking very fast. He had been involved in a fight at a club in New York. The other guy had hit him first, but Henry was the one with the knife.

"A knife?" I said.

"I was only defending myself," Henry said. "I had no choice."

The police, fortunately, had not been called, but the club's manager was holding Henry in custody until someone came and picked him up. The other boy had been taken to the hospital.

"Will you come get me?" Henry said.

"I think you should call your father," I said.

"My father hates me," Henry said. "He'd leave me here to rot."

I could not believe that Hart hated his son, even a son like Henry, but there was something in the boy's voice that made me want to help him, or at the very least frightened me enough so that I thought I should help him. I wrote down the club's address and told Henry I would be there soon.

Before I left, George and I had a terrible fight, our first since moving into our new house.

"You're not going out in the middle of the night to pick up some stranger," George said.

"Henry is not a stranger. He's our neighbor," I said.

"He's not a good neighbor," George said. "He's not the kind of neighbor I want you to be friends with."

"You were the one who wanted to move out here, out of the city," I said. "I thought you would be so happy."

"I thought you would be happy too," George said.

We stopped for a moment and looked at each other. Then I began to get dressed, pulling on my jeans and an old pink sweater I had owned since high school that always made me feel safe and strong.

"I said you're not going," George said. He had been in bed, but he got out and stood in front of me while I tried to put on my shoes. As I rose, he took hold of my wrists and held them both tight. "It's ten o'clock at night, for God's sake," he said.

"I have to help him," I said, and felt, just as I had so many times before, that I really did have to help this young man out.

"You're not going," George said.

"You can't tell me what to do," I said, and I broke free from his hold.

Then we really started to scream at each other. George called me names I had never been called before, and at one point he picked up the book he had been reading throughout the week and threw it hard against the wall. He wanted to throw it at me, I am sure, and he nearly did.

"You're driving me crazy," George said. He slapped his hands against his head with a smack.

"I hate you," I said, although at this point I could barely remember why our fight had begun.

"Get out of here," George said, and then of course I did.

The club where Henry was being held captive was on the Lower East Side of Manhattan. It was crowded when I arrived; there was a line of young people waiting outside and there was no place to park the car. Besides, George had not yet taught me to parallel park, and the thought of even attempting it without prior instruction left me bewildered. I ended up leaving the Toyota on the corner in an illegal spot, its rear jutting out in the street.

The manager's office was smoke-filled and dark, and there appeared to be a fine layer of grease over all the furniture in the room. Henry sat in the corner, dressed similarly as the day before. He looked at me blank-faced when I walked in, as if he had forgotten who I was, had forgotten that it was he who had called me. Suddenly he grinned.

"You came," he said. "You're something else."

I shrugged.

The manager, a short thin man dressed in tight linen pants and dark glasses, asked me if I was related to

Henry. When I told him I was only his neighbor, he shook his head.

"Oh sugar," he said. "How did he get you to come down?"

The manager told me that he had not called the police due to Henry's young age, but that did not mean the other boy would not press charges. He was in the hospital having five stitches sewn into his cheek.

"It was not a pretty sight," the manager said.

"But he threatened to kill me," Henry said. "I was just defending myself."

"You were the only one with a knife," the manager said, and I had to agree it seemed as if Henry were at greater fault.

"I'll take him home now," I said, and I ushered Henry out of the club, through the throngs of people, into my car.

Once out in the car, Henry became much more animated.

"Boy, this car is beat," he said. "How old is it?"

"It's new for me," I said. I was nervous and stalled twice before getting the Toyota to move into reverse.

"Want me to drive?" Henry asked.

"No," I said. I clenched the wheel tightly and maneuvered out into traffic.

We had only driven a few blocks when Henry pulled out his knife. It was not a particularly large knife, but its blade was sharp, and although it now was clean I imagined it stained red with the blood of the boy from the club. Henry wiped it with a cloth he carried in his back jeans pocket, then closed and opened it a few times.

"There's a real art to using a blade," Henry said as we stopped for a light.

"I'm sure there is," I said. I was thinking of George at

119

home in bed. I was sorry that I had told him I hated him. I did not hate him; I merely felt detached. In our old home in the city there had been my job and the streets of New York and even other men to make me feel a part of the world. Out here in Connecticut there was only George. I knew he thought I was willing myself not to get pregnant, as if my body was unable to betray my mind and heart. But he was wrong; I wanted a baby now, a child. If only for company on those long stretches of days ahead.

Henry was pushing the blade of his knife into the dashboard of my car. There were already two slices along the edge.

"Please don't do that," I said. "You're making holes in the car."

"The car is already beat," Henry said.

"At any rate, I would like you to stop." The streets were crowded and I found myself stuck in the middle of an intersection behind a cab. Cars behind me honked on their horns.

"Who's going to make me?" Henry said, and, grinning, he flicked the knife in my direction. "I could kill you, you know," he suddenly said. His high-pitched voice grew even higher.

I swerved to the left of the cab, missing its side door by inches. "I'm trying to drive," I said.

"I said I could kill you," Henry said. "I know how."

I tried to remain calm and concentrate on my driving, but the lights at each intersection seemed to threaten me with danger. The steering wheel felt sticky under my palms and I discovered I wasn't even sure where I was, how to get back home. I hoped I was headed north.

All at once, with a quick darting motion, Henry shoved the blade of the knife just below my chin.

"Pull over," he whispered.

"I can't," I said, nearly letting go of the wheel altogether, nearly closing my eyes.

Henry pushed the blade of the knife against my skin and I felt a small sharp pain, like the prick of the needle when giving blood. "Pull over," he said.

Quickly, I made my way through the traffic and pulled over to a side street, stopping the car somewhere between the curb and the middle of the road. I left the ignition and lights on.

Henry was nearly on top of me now. "I could rape you, you know," he said, tugging at my pink sweater. "I could rape you right here in your stupid beat-up car." He kept the knife poised at my chin. I could feel a small drop of blood, like perspiration, trickle down my throat.

"Please stop," I said, and I would not let go of the steering wheel. "Please just let me take you home."

"Who's going to make me?" Henry said. He had gotten one of his hands inside my pink sweater and I could feel it at my breast.

"Stop it," I said. Then, without really thinking, on instinct alone, I let go of the steering wheel and with my free hand I slapped Henry across the face. It was probably not hard enough to really hurt him but it did startle him, and he let go of me instantly, pulled the knife to his chest, and then started to cry. His face looked pale and thin in the dark car. His short orange hair pressed against the closed window. He looked almost ten years younger than he had only moments ago.

"I wasn't going to really rape you," he said. His voice was high and he trembled, he was crying so hard.

"That's not what you told me," I said.

"I was just kidding around," he said.

"It wasn't funny," I said.

Then, still crying, he said, "I've never been with a

girl. I just wanted to see if you would do it." He closed up his knife and put it back in his pocket. "I'm sorry, but I'm fifteen and I've never been with a girl before. Girls don't like me," he said.

"No wonder," I said.

"I just wanted to see what it felt like," he said.

"That's not my problem," I said, and I was already thinking ahead about where I was and how to get home. I also thought about George, and how, despite myself, I always felt safe with him, very safe.

"You don't know what it's like living with my father," Henry said, and his entire body heaved with his sobs. "He's crazy. He wants me to iron my underwear."

"Tough shit," I said. Reaching over him, I opened the car door, and with a quick shove pushed him out onto the street. He fell with a thud.

"Hey," I heard him say, but I quickly locked the door. I stalled a few times before getting the car into gear, then drove away. However, I did look back once through the rearview mirror, feeling something almost like pity for Henry in the street behind me.

I drove for a few blocks; I was on Third Avenue going uptown, but I did not know how to get back to the new house in Connecticut. I could not remember the street address, or even the town.

Finally I pulled over to a phone and dialed George. I did, at least, remember my telephone number. I let the phone ring almost thirty times, and then, fearing I had the wrong number, I dialed again. Although it was nearly two, there was no answer. George had to be home. I called again, but still no one answered. Perhaps he knew it was me and was not answering out of spite. Or perhaps George was sleeping soundly.

I put the receiver down and peered out of the dirty

glass of the telephone booth into the street. Except for the cars, the sidewalks were empty, the streets were quiet. I felt very alone and abandoned and I began to play a game I had not played since I was a child. I pretended that I had magical powers and that if I thought hard enough I would be whisked away to anywhere in the world. At the age of five I had gone to places like Disneyland and our house at the beach. At a somewhat older age I had traveled to Europe and also to San Francisco, where a boy I had fallen in love with the summer before had moved. Now, however, when I closed my eyes I did not know where I wanted to go. The magical powers were still with me, but the places of adventure or safety or love seemed to no longer exist.

It was my father who finally took me home. First back to his apartment to spend the night, and then the next morning all the way back to Connecticut.

"This is something I would expect from your brother, not from you," my father said to me as we drove out of the city. But he did not sound angry. "You were always so level-headed, Annie."

"I guess I'm slipping," I said. I hoped I wasn't slipping too far.

The Connecticut house was empty when we arrived, and though my father offered to stay with me, I drove him to the train station and waved him on his way.

"Remember this, Annie," my father warned me at the station. "You can only trust your family. Not friends, certainly not neighbors." Then he hugged me tight and boarded the train back to the city.

Back at home, I noticed a note from George taped to the front of our new refrigerator. "Dear Anne," it read. "Call me at work." Then, in smaller print, "I love you."

"You don't even know if I made it home okay," I

shouted at the refrigerator door, as if the handwritten note were George himself. "Perhaps I was killed at knifepoint by a boy named Henry." I kicked the door with my shoe and enjoyed the dark smudge mark it made.

"How could you just leave?" I said, but then even I giggled. It was silly, yelling at a refrigerator, and besides, I was not the type to get killed in a car, to not make it home. George knew that and had gone to work just the same. Standing now in the bright kitchen, the events of last night no longer seemed dangerous, hardly threatening at all. There had always been cars and people and lights; perhaps there had been no risk. Soon, I knew this episode with Henry would slowly become no more real than so many other events in my life, the ones that over time become such good stories that I imagine I have read them, or heard them told at a party by some other girl, a girl not so level-headed, not so sure.

I did not call George back right away, though I knew later I would. George would say it did not matter about the baby, about getting pregnant, and I would say we should try some more. George would ask if I really hated him, and I would say it was impossible to hate a man like him. It would be true. Then he would say he would be home in just a few hours, and of course he would show up on time.

Now, though, while it was still early, I walked outside and looked over to my neighbor's yard. I do not know what I expected, but the yard was as before. The various flowers, the shrubs, the vegetable garden in the back. Hart, in his yellow hat, was even weeding the flower bed closest to the house. He pulled out a few weeds, placed them into the trash bag he carried with him, then wiped his hands on the front of his shorts. When he heard me, he looked up and smiled.

124

"Anne," he called. "Always a pleasure."

"How are you doing?" I said.

"Feeling better to see your pretty face," he said. Then Hart waved his garbage bag in the air. "Anne," he called again. "Come over for a chat. I've got some fresh tomatoes for you just ripe for the picking." Hart waved the bag again. "Come on over."

I like to think humans learn from their mistakes, but we are creatures of circumstance, and certainly habit, and so of course I walked over to my neighbor's yard. I waved hello, we talked, I fetched the tomatoes.

SMALL ACTS
OF VIOLENCE

The party was a disaster. Our host and hostess argued early on—something to do with his mother, who was caring for their ten-year-old daughter. The Middle Eastern food was terrible, and the punch was weak. If it were my house, my party, I would also have been disappointed with the showing. Only four other couples came and two left early, one woman claiming a headache, the other a babysitter that could not stay past midnight. George, who has a sympathetic nature, insisted that we stay far later than either of us would have liked.

"Look at Lydia," George said, referring to our hostess. "She looks absolutely green."

George even complimented Lydia on the dip, which I knew he had not even tasted, and he helped Alan, Lydia's husband, refill the punch bowl.

As it turned out, we were the last ones to leave the party. Since we only lived up the block and could walk home, Alan kept refreshing our drinks with less and less ice, and sometime around one he even lit up a joint.

"Do either of you smoke pot?" Alan asked.

George shook his head no, I too passed, and Lydia shrugged.

"Well, I do," Alan said, and he inhaled deeply. Then, looking at his wife, "I shouldn't have to hide it at my age."

"Not on our account," I said.

Alan smiled. "You are someone I could get to like," he said to me.

Neither George nor I knew what to say then, and there was an uncomfortable silence while each of us looked around for the other to speak.

George, who is always courteous, finally did. "It's going to be a beautiful autumn. The weather must be just right for the foliage."

"I don't get into that crap myself," Alan said. "A leaf is a leaf."

"It's a pity you have all those leaves right in your backyard," I said to him. "What a waste."

Alan laughed. "You're really funny," he said.

"No, I'm not," I said. I had not been trying to be funny. I began collecting used napkins from the end tables, from the arm of the couch, even from the floor.

"Yes, you are," Alan said. "I've noticed that all evening. How funny you are. George, you have a very funny wife."

"Thank you," George said.

"And a very pretty wife," Alan said. "I've never seen such beautiful blue eyes."

"Thank you," George said again.

127

Then we all fell silent, listening to Alan inhale and the sound of the stereo playing the Allman Brothers, and soon after Lydia and I began to clean up the party remains.

I was not in the living room when the fight broke out; I was in the kitchen helping Lydia load the dishwasher, rinse the lipstick stains out of the good glasses. Lydia and I were chatting about a petition that had recently been sent around requesting alternate-side-of-the-street parking in the town.

"I sign everything on principle," Lydia was saying. "I'm sure I agree with at least half of what I sign."

Suddenly we heard a yelp, like the sound a dog makes when its tail gets stuck in the door. It was Alan. "You son of a bitch," he said. Then there was a loud scuffle, and by the time we reached the two men the punch bowl had been overturned on top of Alan's head.

"I hope you taste that horrible punch of yours for days," George said. Then, upon seeing Lydia and me, he blushed and stuttered a quick apology.

"What's going on?" I said.

And Lydia, as if she had done or seen this before, deftly removed the bowl from Alan's head, hung the ladle on the bowl's edge, and placed it back on the table. Alan groaned. The red-brown liquid was dripping down his face onto the collar of his shirt, and he held his head as if he had been wounded, cracked across the skull, and the punch were his own blood.

"Son of a bitch," Alan said. "We're just sitting here talking and next thing I know he's dumping the punch over my head."

Lydia looked around the room, at the stain that was spreading across the carpet, at the cigarettes stubbed dead into her end table, and then back at her husband. I saw her face crumple like a piece of paper, but she did not cry. Instead she led Alan into the kitchen to clean up.

"If we wash that shirt in cold water right away, the stain will come out," she said, and Alan followed her without a word.

"What happened?" I said to George as soon as we were alone. He had already gone to get our coats. "How could you do such a thing?"

George helped me on with my coat, smoothing my hair in the back so that it did not catch in my collar. He patted it then, as if to reassure a small child, or a puppy.

"That man is not very nice," George finally said. "I suggest you stay far away from him, Anne."

If George had been another man I might have imagined Alan had made some suggestive comment about me. His kiss had certainly been a little too friendly upon our arrival, and he kept touching me all evening, on my hand when he offered me a drink, on my chin when I told a story. But George has never been a jealous man. That kind of talk, even that kind of kiss, does not bother George. It must have been something else that Alan had said or done, but I could not imagine what.

In the kitchen I waved good-bye to Lydia and Alan. "We really must be going," I said to them. They were both standing in front of the sink, like modern lifelike sculpture, they were so still. Alan had not yet washed; his hair was matted flat against his forehead, his shirt was soaked red. Lydia shrugged when she saw me, but did not speak.

"Thank you for the party," I said to her, and to Alan, "Sorry about your shirt."

Alan, very strangely, blew me a kiss. Then George and I left the house together.

It had grown colder over the course of the evening

and George and I huddled close together as we walked the short block back home. The leaves from the trees above us made strange shadows on the sidewalk—some looked like the outlines of animals, others looked like faces I had known. Our breath made smoke in front of our mouths, and George took my hand inside his pocket and held it there as we walked.

"You don't have to tell me," I said to him just before we reached the light of our porch. "But I wish you would."

"I wish you wouldn't ask me right now," George said. "I feel foolish enough as it is."

"Don't feel bad," I said. "He really is a creep."

"I thought they were your friends," George said.

"Hardly," I said. Then, because we were out of that house and away from those people, I thought of Alan's face, the look he made when the punch bowl was removed from his head, and I laughed.

"What's so funny?" George said.

"The way Alan looked with that bowl on his head," I said. "And that horrible punch."

"Not so funny," George said. Then he took my chin in his hands and kissed me on the lips. When I shivered he asked me if I was cold.

"Not too," I said. Then we slowed our pace even more, and it seemed a long time before we finally reached home.

The next morning, after I had driven George to the train station, Lydia called to apologize.

"I know it was awful," she said. Her voice was low and slightly hoarse, as if she had been smoking too many cigarettes or had just awakened. "I hope you'll forgive us and still be our friend."

I was somewhat surprised; I had never considered

Lydia a friend and had not imagined she considered me one, either. She and I had talked occasionally, as neighbors will, and because we were a good bit younger than most of our other neighbors there was a certain generational bond. We talked about our college days, and about my old job in the city, and sometimes she spoke of her daughter, Amanda. But nothing that would qualify us as friends.

"I guess George told you what Alan said," Lydia continued.

"No, he didn't," I said.

"Oh," said Lydia. If it were me, if I were Lydia, I would have left it right there; I would have spoke of other things. What goes on between a husband and wife should not be explained or interpreted by family or friends, and certainly not by neighbors. Their secrets should not be revealed. But Lydia is another kind of woman. Alan had shamelessly told her what had happened, and she eagerly repeated it to me.

Last night, right before George dumped the bowl over Alan's head, Alan had recommended himself to George as a surrogate father. Alan had heard somehow, from someone, that George and I could not have children together, that we had been trying for a long while and were not successful.

"Let me do it for you," Alan had said. "I'm sure it would only take once. Just one good shot."

"He said that?" I said to Lydia.

"A wise man lets another man do what he cannot," Alan had continued.

"I can't believe he actually said that," I said.

"I am sure he was only joking," Lydia said.

"Does he often joke that way?" I said.

"Well, I know he didn't really mean it," Lydia said. "I'm sure it was because of all that he had drunk."

"Not much of an excuse," I said.

"Well, George was the one who spilled the punch over Alan's head," Lydia said.

"With good reason, it appears," I said.

"I'm sure you don't really feel that way," Lydia said, and then, "Let's not let this one incident stand in the way of a good friendship."

"How can it not?" I said, and then for some reason I told Lydia I would be glad to pay for the cleaning—the shirt, the carpet—to just drop the bill in my mail, and without even saying good-bye I hung up.

George was sad for days after the party. When he came home from work he had little appetite for dinner. Instead of eating he would go upstairs to our bedroom and either watch television from our bed or go to sleep. He stopped shaving and wore the same yellow tie to work three days in a row. He began to grow thin. I tried to talk to him about it. I suggested we try another fertility doctor, but George would not hear of it.

"Look," he said to me. "I don't want to be one of those desperate couples that go from doctor to doctor, putting their faith in every new drug or method that comes along. Sometimes one must believe in fate, Anne, that if God had meant for you and me to have children together he would have made sure that we could."

George then slept for twelve hours straight. Later, I tried telling him that it did not matter, that I had never been keen on having children in the first place, but this only made him sadder. Finally I let him be, and ironically after a week he seemed cured. We forgot all about the terrible party. Lydia and I ignored each other in the supermarket, and only nodded if we passed one another on the street. George's appetite returned, he began to care again for the way he bathed and dressed.

"I'm glad you're feeling better about things," I said to George as he readied himself for work. He was putting the stays in the collar of his shirt; it was white and crisp and made me think of fresh laundry drying on a line, of starting anew. "You seem happy again," I said.

"I realize there is nothing I can do about it," George said. "Let people say what they will—I cannot have children."

"But we can always practice," I said.

George grinned, and when we kissed he ran his fingers all the way down my back. "I intend to," he said.

Three weeks later, however, something strange happened that reminded me of the fight between Alan and George—unexpected and wrong. I had gone at six-thirty to pick George up from the station, just as I always did. But when I arrived George was not waiting for me at the curb, and there was a crowd of people standing in front of the train, which had not yet pulled out for its next stop. When the crowd separated I saw George being held on the arm by one of the train conductors.

"Anne," George called out when he saw me.

"Is this man your husband?" the conductor asked me.

"Of course," I said, and only then did he let go of George, shaking his hands as he did so. "What happened?" I said.

"He tripped a man disembarking from the train," the conductor said. "On purpose. He stuck his leg out at the level of the man's knees."

"He did this on purpose?" I asked.

"I didn't like the way he was looking at me," said George.

"I don't like you," the conductor said.

"I didn't even hurt him," George said.

133

"You could have broken every bone in the man's body," the conductor said. He then took his blue cap off his head and ran his fingers through his hair. He made a whistling sound through his teeth. Then, replacing his cap, he said, "Your husband is lucky. The man decided not to press charges. But he could have, and he could have walked away with a bundle."

"I'm terribly sorry," I said. "I'm certain it was an accident."

"No," George said, "it wasn't." But I was already leading him away to the waiting car.

Although I tried many times, we did not talk about what had happened at the station; George did not want to and could not be persuaded to tell me why he had deliberately tripped a stranger who to my knowledge had done nothing to George. Perhaps it could even have been forgotten, but it turned out not to be an isolated occurrence. George, for no apparent reason, started performing small acts of violence.

On Saturday, I found him out in the backyard clubbing a groundhog with a large stick. The poor creature was so badly beaten I had to take it to the vet in a box to be put to sleep. Another day, I found George hanging out our second-floor window throwing stones he had collected at passing cars. George was like a child who was doing something he knew was wrong, and was finding great delight in doing so.

"You could be arrested," I told him.

"Don't worry," he said to me. "I haven't hit a car yet."

I even received a call from a colleague of George's, a lawyer who worked closely with him. It appeared that George had decked an opposing attorney in the boardroom.

"The man's nose was bloodied," George's colleague

told me over the phone. "And his pride was hurt. Let's hope he doesn't sue."

"I'm sorry," I said.

"What's strange," the man continued, "is that the blow was completely without provocation. George hit him for no reason at all. What's gotten into him, Anne?"

"I'll talk to him," I said to appease the man, but I could not imagine what I would say.

Clearly, George and I have had our problems. There were the other men (though I considered them well in my past), and George has worked late and been obsessive about things he could not change. Now, of course, there was no child—George cringed each time he saw a father with a baby and cried at the most inane of television family dramas. But never in all the time I have known him has he been a violent man. He has never struck me, and only on occasion thrown things at me. George believed in dealing with anger in a calm, rational manner.

"That is why I became a lawyer," he had often told me.

George was kind to animals, and children were attracted to him. He had an unusual rapport with them that they naturally liked; at the beach and at parks, children surrounded George like horseflies. But now, for some reason, out of nowhere George had become mean. If a storekeeper even looked at him just a moment too long, George would begin to shout, ranting about poor service, shoddy merchandise. He chased Henry off our backyard twice. And at dinner, merely because the soup had turned lukewarm, George threw his bowl across the room. Bits of vegetable and chicken broth ran down our white walls. I did not know what to say to him, how to deal with his anger, and I called Walter for advice.

"Is that the same George we all know and love so well?" Walter said over the phone.

"You wouldn't recognize him," I said.

"Could be a blessing in disguise," Walter said.

"Walter," I said. "He acts like a madman."

"Sounds as if the guy has snapped," Walter said.

"Snapped?" I said.

"Lost it, gone under. Loony tunes," said Walter.

"You think he's crazy?" I said.

"I've always thought that," Walter said.

"Do be serious," I said.

Finally Walter recognized the urgency in my voice; he turned off the radio that had been playing in the background and put the receiver close to his mouth.

"I think he's had some kind of mental breakdown," Walter said.

"What should I do?" I said.

"Come into the city and stay with me," said Walter, and he meant it. "I'll protect you from that lunatic."

"He is not a lunatic," I said.

"Annie," Walter said.

"I just know George better than you," I said, but I was not so sure.

"I just hope you don't get hurt," Walter said, and though we hung up soon afterwards, Walter began calling me twice a week. "Just to make sure your husband hasn't burned down the house," Walter would say, and I certainly appreciated hearing his familiar voice.

I believe the patterns in a marriage are established early on, and sometimes it takes much more than infidelity, or depression, or even tragedy to disturb these patterns. I am ashamed now to say that despite the change in George's behavior, our own life together changed very little. I do not remember fearing for my own safety, and if I worried that George might seriously harm someone else I kept it hidden. I did not call any doctors, did not recommend that George take a vacation from work. I suppose I asked him on more than one occasion what was troubling him, but he always said nothing. One evening, after I found him tearing up his family's photograph album, I even asked him about children.

"We could adopt a child," I suggested to him. Pieces of his mother and father, of his younger sister, lay scattered over the carpet like shards of glass. I gathered them all together and let them fall back inside the pages of the album, an arm here, a face there, a Christmas tree in the binding. "It would be just like our own child," I said.

"It wouldn't be anything like our own child," George said. "I know it's selfish, but that's the way I feel. It wouldn't have my hair, my eyes, my blood."

"But you could still play with the child, still care for it," I said. I put my arms around George and tried to pull him close to my chest, but he resisted.

"A man dies and wants to leave something behind in the world," George said very softly. "I'm not leaving anything behind."

"You're also not dying," I said. I rubbed his back, felt his spine and the muscles of his shoulders. It was all familiar, warm.

"Anne," said George finally. "There is so much you don't know about me."

"I'd like to know," I said.

"But you won't," he said.

"I see," I said.

"It's okay," George said.

But everything was not okay. His bizarre behavior continued. If someone today asked me, I would not be able to tell them why I allowed it to go on so long. It may be as simple as the fact that George was my husband and my loyalty to him precluded my loyalty to the outside world. Or perhaps I just liked our life together—there was so much that I could count on. I knew each day I would drive George to the station and then pick him up again in the evening. I knew I would spend my mornings running errands or cleaning the house. In the afternoons I might go into the city and visit with a friend or stop by at one of the museums. I might garden or try my hand at poetry or knitting. At night George and I would watch the news for half an hour and then more often than not make love. If not completely happy, I was not unhappy, either, and despite George's fearful actions, I found our life together comforting.

It was at another party, this time at my father's apartment, that George's violence broke out again. Just as Walter had diagnosed, George really did seem to snap.

We were all eating dinner in the dining room. Though it usually seemed cold and sterile to me because of its size, this day, with my family gathered together, the room was suddenly intimate and warm. The dining room table had been polished and set with silver, tall candlesticks, flowers, and the good china. Isabelle had prepared roast lamb and minty potatoes. There was lemon meringue pie for dessert.

"An Easter feast," my father had proclaimed, although Easter was still weeks away. Then, raising his glass, my father toasted us all.

It was just the family—my father and Isabelle, Walter, George, and me. Yvette, now thirteen, was home from school and she sat next to George, saying and eating very little. There was also Isabelle's new son, Gregory. He was just two and sat in a high chair near my father at the head of the table. We had all laughed at his antics during the meal. Twice he had grabbed food from my father's plate. He spilled his milk once. Each time we laughed, he of course giggled and called out our names for approval.

"You're only encouraging him to misbehave," Yvette said at one point.

"Lighten up," her mother said. "We let you do the same thing when you were his age."

"Like hell," Yvette said. She pushed her pie around her plate with the tines of her fork. She looked at George and pouted.

"We let you get away with it now," said my father, laughing, and though he winked at Yvette, she did not smile back.

Just then, Gregory took aim and threw a piece of his pie across the table. I do not know if he had aimed for her, but the lemon meringue squarely hit Yvette in the head. Gregory seemed to know that he had gone a bit too far. He looked down at his shirt and then at his mother, pursing his small lips and then actually trying a smile.

"Gregory," Isabelle said, but without conviction.

Yvette glared at her mother. "You let him get away with everything," she said. Then, turning to Gregory, she said, "I hate you." With her napkin she struggled to pull the sticky clump of meringue out of her hair, but it stuck fast near her forehead. "I hate you," she screamed.

"You don't hate him," my father said good-humoredly.

"I hate his little guts," Yvette said. "He's a spoiled brat who gets everything he wants. I wish he had never been born."

It was then that George lost it. He might have been more sympathetic with Yvette. After all, sibling rivalry is nothing new and she had been her mother's only child for eleven years. It was natural for her to feel some resentment. And, if truth be known, Gregory was spoiled. But George, who had always been so sensitive to Yvette's feelings in the past, who had been her favorite, even, showed no sensitivity or gentleness at all. He sprung from the table, yanked Yvette's arm, and swung her off her chair with a sharp twist. I heard a small pop as her arm dislocated from her shoulder, and Yvette began to scream.

"Don't you talk about your brother that way," George said to her, and his knuckles were white from holding her so tight. "Be thankful, bless God every day that he was born at all."

By this time my father was struggling to pull George away. It was with great difficulty. George is a large man and also quite a bit younger than my father. Nevertheless, Yvette was finally released. Isabelle had gone to call an ambulance and bring an ice pack for Yvette's arm. Walter soothed her, called Yvette pretty names, patted her head, took her in his arms. Oblivious to us all, Gregory continued to eat his pie.

At my family's insistence I admitted George into a hospital for two week's observation. And I moved in with my father and Isabelle.

"I don't want you in that big old house all alone," my father said to me. "You stay with us."

I was only too glad to comply.

Since Yvette was confined to her bed by the doctor and needed care, I helped Isabelle watch over Gregory. He was an active child. He would climb out of his crib at six in the morning and clamber into my room.

"Annie," he would say, tugging at my arm or hair, "let's play."

We did play together; I took him for walks in the park, gave him his afternoon bath, and made soap bubbles, or clay figures, or water color drawings to keep him amused. In only a few days we became fast friends. He made his mother move his chair next to mine at the dinner table, and he begged me instead of my father for bedtime stories. I would tuck him in so that the covers went up to his chin, and then, sitting in a chair beside his crib I would read to him from Dr. Seuss or the adventures of Babar the elephant. He knew most of the stories, and would sometimes chime in with me until he grew too weary and his eyes would flutter and close.

I must admit I was flattered by Gregory's attention, and also surprised at how quickly his attachment for me had grown. When he called my name, or threw his arms around my knees, I felt an unusual tug inside. Sometimes it could make me cry.

There is little anyone can say to soften the blow. My husband had a nervous breakdown. I had to explain it to his associates at work and I had to call his mother in New Hampshire and give her the news.

"What have you done to him?" she said, and I did indeed often wonder during George's stay in the hospital whether it was something I had caused, or something I could have prevented. But when I visited him in the hospital, I oddly hoped that the doctors would not let George out too soon.

As it turned out, George's stay in the hospital lasted more than three months. I went home only to fetch some clothes and a few personal effects. I told no one where I was going, and since I had few friends in Connecticut I did not expect any calls from people wondering where I was, why our lights were always off, why our paper was not being picked up. It was after the first month, however, that I did receive a call from a neighbor. It came in the evening, just as I was returning to my father's apartment from visiting George. It was my neighbor Lydia.

"You sure are hard to track down," Lydia said in her hoarse voice.

Though later it puzzled me, I did not even ask how she had found me. Instead I asked why she was calling at all.

"I was worried about you," she said. "Your house was dark, and Hart said he hadn't seen you or George in weeks. I haven't seen you go out to pick up your mail."

"We're taking a vacation," I said. Isabelle, who was in the kitchen with me, was making soup. She looked at me, narrowed her eyes, and smiled.

"Get real," said Lydia.

"Actually," I said, "George has been sick. I'm staying here until he recuperates."

Lydia did not hesitate, did not pause to think about what she was saying. "Sick?" she said. "Look, Anne, the whole town knows George has been having some problems."

I am not sure why I did not hang up on her right then. Perhaps it was because Isabelle was there, straining her broth, listening. Or perhaps I was curious that Lydia had bothered to call at all.

"He's getting much better," I said.

"I certainly hope so," Lydia said. "We have all been worried about you, and of course George, too." For a moment I thought she actually meant it, might have cared in some strange way, and I could almost picture myself returning to Connecticut, entering the door of my castle, sleeping in my own bed.

But then Lydia spoke again. "Speaking only as a friend," she began, "I could tell from the moment I met you and George that you were both unsuited, short-lived. That he was crazy, you were sane."

I heard Gregory in the next room. "Annie," he called. Then he came walking in. His shoelaces were untied, his hands and mouth were covered with blue paint.

"Gregory," I said, shaking my head.

Lydia continued over the telephone. "You should leave George," she said to me. "Go out on your own. You're young and pretty. Believe me, you'll have no trouble. No trouble at all. . . ."

"I've got to go," I said, and I hung up before she finished speaking, before she could say any more.

I cleaned Gregory of the paint with a cloth and soap, tied his shoelaces, and kissed him on the cheek. I tasted Isabelle's soup and told her it was perfect. I even ran down the hall to see how Yvette was faring, to talk to her about schoolwork, boys. I did not think I cared another minute about Lydia's call, about what she had said. I told Isabelle it was certainly nothing. But late that night, as I lay in the bed that had been set up for me in the study, I kept hearing Lydia's words over and over—unsuited, short-lived, crazy. Strangely, there among my father's books in the dark, I feared her words might be true.

George's room in the hospital was barren; no one had sent him flowers or cards, there were no children on his floor, and the other patients stayed in their own rooms, sometimes making strange noises at night. There were, however, baskets of food Isabelle had prepared and given me to bring in, and Walter had brought in an armload of new books. Even my father, who is slow to forgive, had replaced the small black-and-white hospital television with a larger, color TV. And that is how I often found George, watching television from his bed, flicking the channels with his remote control.

"I know you're angry I brought you to the hospital," I said to him one evening. It was only a few days before he was scheduled to come home. "But I didn't think I had a choice."

143

"I'm sure you didn't," George said. The television switched from *Wheel of Fortune* to *Jeopardy*. I turned it off, but George turned it back on. I sat down on the edge of his bed. I had thought a long time about what I was going to say to him. I had talked it over with my father and Walter. I had even rehearsed on little Gregory, practicing my lines so seriously in the park that I made him laugh, and then cough.

"I hate to tell you this here," I began. Alex Trebek was explaining the different categories on *Jeopardy*. One was "Lost Loves." "But I want everything understood before you are released," I said.

"I can't agree more," said George.

"I think we should separate," I said. It was out. George had heard. "Not necessarily divorce," I added. "But go our separate ways."

George nodded, and I took his hand in my own. Then I lay down next to him on the narrow hospital bed and, touching the control button, I lowered us so that we were lying nearly flat.

"I don't think we are good for each other," I continued. "I don't think we make each other happy."

"You don't make me unhappy," George whispered in my ear.

I looked into his face. He did not look like a healthy man. His skin was pale and his eyebrows appeared almost gray. His hospital robe smelled of antiseptic and even blood. I turned away from him and held my breath. I tried to imagine George out of the hospital, in his own clothes, in our house, perhaps in the backyard mowing the lawn or pulling up weeds. But instead I saw him clubbing the groundhog again. His hand held the stick above his head and when he brought it down upon the creature, I winced.

George moved in the bed, his cold feet touching my legs, but I did not look at him. Instead I told him that we needed to be apart.

"It's for the best," I said.

"I suppose so," said George.

"You can keep the house," I said to him. "That way you'll have a place to go back to when you get out."

"The house?" George said as if he didn't understand.

"And the car," I added.

"Okay," George said. Then, as if the matter was finally resolved, he turned back to look at the TV. A woman on *Jeopardy* had just won eight thousand dollars and there was loud applause. The woman was smiling and shaking the other contestants' hands. George punched the television control to another station and then to another, and another.

"I can never find anything to watch on TV," he said. "The programs are never what you expect."

Then he began to cry. He kept punching the remote control on the television, the stations flickered in and out, and he cried so hard that his whole body shuddered.

"Anne," said George, "I can't find anything I like."

"I can't either," I said.

I took the control away from him and placed it on the table. Then, taking his head into my arms, I listened to him sob. The world was not a friendly place for George, nor did it seem so then to me. I knew I did not even have the heart to leave.

THE PART THAT'S LOST

There were family at my mother's funeral I had never met before. Not just aunts and uncles and cousins, although there were plenty of them, but brothers and sisters, even a stepfather.

A ten-year-old half-sister laid lily of the valley on my mother's grave site. With her reddish blond hair, her freckles, she looked astonishingly like my mother. Much more so than me. She was a lovely girl even in her somber blue dress and black patent leather shoes. A photographer might have snapped her picture as she bit her lip and twisted one finger far too roughly through her hair. A YOUNG GIRL IN GRIEF, the photographer might have called it. I had never even been told of the girl's birth, but our eyes, particularly on this day, were so much alike I had to turn away.

There were two half-brothers as well, older and less apparently related to me than their sister. They were darker, like their father, and tall for their age. The one I supposed to be the younger of the two had twisted loose his tie at the knot, and as we spoke he kept touching his neck above his shirt, not as if he had an itch, but as if he were afraid his neck might altogether disappear. As the boys introduced themselves to me, shaking my hand—smiling, even—they paused, waiting for me to offer the customary expression of sympathy. As if she hadn't been my mother, too.

"Thank you for coming," they said to me, and after a few more perfunctory words they returned to their father, a large balding man in an ill-fitting suit. His small eyes were reddened but kind, and he looked as if any small breeze, wrong word, would send him toppling over.

A moment later the older and more handsome brother turned around to me and said, "It was nice to meet you finally. Too bad it had to be for this."

I nodded politely and watched the boy take his father's arm, holding it tight.

I tried to imagine this man, my stepfather, with my mother. He had been there in the car with her when it crashed, may even have watched her die. It was she who had been driving, though. I had heard my father say that the coroner had reported a heavy alcohol content in her blood.

"She liked to have a good time," my father had added.

But for some reason I do not remember my mother ever laughing. I cannot picture her smiling, even, though perhaps with her second husband she smiled all the time. Maybe they were returning from a party where they had danced and laughed frequently throughout the night. They

147

had shared glasses of champagne and toasted to each other's enjoyment. The man had escorted my mother to the car. She had insisted on driving, of course, and they kissed not once, but many times before pulling away. I would like to think my mother had at least died happy.

Perhaps all these thoughts were to assuage my guilt. I almost had not come to the funeral at all.

"I do not owe her anything," I had told my father. "What kind of mother was she ever to me?"

The last time I had seen my mother was at my own wedding. She had barely spoken to me—only twice throughout the day, once to complain about her corsage and then again after the ceremony at the reception. She had told me not to expect much from marriage.

"I'm afraid you have your father's romantic spirit," she had said to me. "I hope you won't be disappointed." Then she brushed a loose hair out of my face and straightened my veil. She did not kiss the bride.

Before the wedding, it had been ten years. I do not remember missing my mother during that time, though perhaps I did—At mother-daughter events at school, on my birthdays, when I went out on my first date, received my first kiss. Only I do not think I was missing her—my mother and I had never been close—but was instead missing the mother I wished I had. And that was probably who I was mourning, as well.

It was my father who finally convinced me to go to the funeral.

"If you don't go you will feel disloyal," he had said to me. Loyalty was of the utmost importance to my father. He advocated loyalty to one's family and to one's self, even to one's school or job.

"Disloyal," my father continued. "You don't want that to ever be said of you." Of course I did not.

My father was not far from the grave site, talking to Walter and a distant relative. When my father caught my eye he waved, and soon after I saw him nudge my brother in my direction. Perhaps they each sensed my loneliness, and Walter was soon at my side.

"Did you meet them all?" he asked me, referring of course to the two half-brothers and half-sister, the stepfather. These relations of marriage, not blood.

I nodded.

"Serious bunch," Walter said. "Don't you think?"

"It's a funeral," I reminded him. "They're supposed to be serious."

"Oh yeah," he said, but I was not convinced.

Walter waved at an older man I did not know and smiled at a pretty girl cousin who flirted back. He made it seem as if he were at a party, as if he was not only comfortable being there, but was actually having a good time.

I shook my head at him. "I feel as if I've crashed it," I said. "Crashed the funeral. And they are all waiting for me to do something frightful, like tell loud off-color jokes or limericks over the grave. I feel as if I don't belong here."

"But she was our mother first," Walter said, as if it really mattered in what order we were all born. He put his arm around me and squeezed my shoulders. "She knew us long before she ever knew them."

"But she never left them," I said. That meant she had loved them more.

"She has left them now," Walter said. Then we both looked on together as they lowered our mother into the ground.

I would like to say my mother's death affected me in some profound way, made me face mortality, made me finally an adult. But in truth, her death affected me hardly at all. Perhaps it was because I had not seen her in so many years, although more likely it was because I merely had other matters on my mind. It was two weeks since I had left George. Left him lying alone in the psychiatric ward of the hospital, watching television, one game show after another. He was back in our house in Connecticut now. I had heard he was even returning to work in a week, though I had not called. Just one brief note letting him know that my mother had died, that I still wished him well.

I was living with Walter in his apartment in New York. My bed was a fold-out couch in the living room and I stored my one suitcase on top of the refrigerator. Walter had told me to bring more clothes, some of my things from home, but I couldn't bear to believe that any of this was permanent. It was such a small apartment, and though Walter and I were close it was probably fortunate that he was rarely home.

Walter worked nights at a drug/suicide hotline and during the day he was one of the many young directors at a local radio station. I only saw Walter at breakfast and sometimes between jobs, though he usually went out for dinner then with some young woman. I had even met a few of his girlfriends and often accused Walter of having met them through his work—not at the radio station, but at the hotline. The women usually had a glazed look in their faces. Often they were dressed in black.

I had taken back my old job at the bookstore. It seemed to be all that I was skilled for, and it reminded me of happier times. My boss at the bookstore warned me, however, that I had lost all seniority and would spend most of my day in the storeroom, but I said I didn't mind. As long as I was busy.

At night I did not usually go out. Instead, I thought often of George, and sometimes I called Walter at work just to hear his comforting voice.

"Atlas Hotline," Walter would answer, soft and reassuring.

"It's only me," I would say.

"Annie," Walter would say. "A breath of sweet sanity."

Then Walter would tell me about the calls he had received so far that night—the man who was trying to drown himself in the bathtub, the woman licking up cocaine. We would talk until the next call came in, then I would hang up feeling I too had been saved. Most often at night, however, I listened to the couple fighting downstairs.

Walter's apartment sat above a laundromat. Because the washing machinery and giant press emitted so much heat, Walter told me he rarely needed to turn on the heat during the winter months and saved on his electric bill. Of course, I reminded him that during the summer the apartment would become oppressively hot. Walter shrugged.

It was a married couple who owned and operated the downstairs laundry. He was a white man named Joe and she was Korean. He called her Rosita. During the day it was Joe who waited on the customers, since Rosita spoke very little English. Instead, she worked in the back giving each shirt an identifying mark, placing the shirts in their correct bins for heavy or light starch, then boxing up those that had been cleaned and pressed in cardboard. Between seven and twelve at night, Joe and Rosita worked the cleaning machinery, large drums that churned the shirts in hot soapy water and a dryer that occupied an entire wall. You would have thought that they were happily married, to work so closely together, but in fact they fought often and loud. Their voices rose above the din of the machinery and into Walter's apartment. It was not that

I could hear their exact words, but the sounds they made—the rising of anger, the shrieks like slaps across the face, and the low rumbling—were far more frightening. Joe cursed loudly in English as he slammed the pressing machine down on each shirt. Rosita screamed in Korean, high-pitched, not human.

"Why do they fight so much?" I asked Walter one morning at breakfast after a particularly loud night. They had kept me awake wondering if George and I had ever fought like that. Also, about violence; was that to become a part of all this, too?

"Actually I once asked Joe," said Walter. He was eating English muffins and the jam had caught on the tip of his chin. He tried to lick it off, but missed and left it there looking like a raspberry birthmark as he took another bite.

"You really asked him?" I said.

Walter nodded, then poured himself a second cup of coffee, letting it spill onto his saucer. Walter was often clumsy like this after a rough night at Atlas Hotline. Last night a seventeen-year-old girl kept him on the phone for almost two hours. She was wondering how barbituates would affect her unborn child.

"Joe said it was because his wife is a stupid foreigner who doesn't know her ass from her elbow," Walter said. He raised his eyebrows, then slurped his coffee. "That's a quote," said Walter.

"I guess that says it all," I said.

"Not really," Walter said. Then, looking at me in a curious way, he said, "It's because they can't have children. I heard them shouting about it one night."

"I see," I said.

"I was with Angela," Walter continued. "Actually she heard it first, but then I heard it too."

I tried to remember who Angela was—I thought she was a blond who wore a huge red bow in her short hair, but I was not sure.

" 'You barren bitch,' is what Joe called her, and some other things too," Walter said. "I'm just quoting," he added.

"Oh," I said.

I wondered how Walter and Angela were able to hear Joe and Rosita's words when I could not. I knew Walter was wondering how I would take this news. There had been other disappointments, of course, but Walter believed, and I did too, that George's inability to have a child was what finally caused him to crack up, what may have ended our marriage even.

"Do you want some more coffee before I go?" Walter asked.

I shook my head. "The whole world is suddenly infertile," I said. Then, looking at the untouched English muffin on my plate, I stabbed it with my fork.

"The city can always use the extra apartment space," Walter said. Neither of us smiled.

After that I found myself listening very carefully to the couple downstairs. I would turn off the television, the radio, and lie across the sofa bed with my head hanging over the side, my ear toward the laundry. At first I found their fights as impossible to decipher as before, but over time I found myself picking up more and more words. I did not hear Joe ever say "barren bitch," but I did hear him say other things to Rosita.

"You're not really a woman," he said to her one night. "You're deformed."

She shrieked back in Korean.

"Maybe you need lessons," he said to her on another occasion. "Maybe you're not doing it right. It sure doesn't feel right to me." His words seemed unusually cruel, and though I do not understand Korean, Rosita's words sounded no kinder. During the worst fights I heard my mother and father have while they were still married, during my worst fights with George, I never heard such hatred. I did not know how the couple could appear so calm and genial during the day.

For I checked on them during the day as well. I offered to take all of Walter's shirts in to be cleaned whenever needed, and sometimes I just peered in on my way to or from work. Joe would be behind the counter as always, smiling and even joking with the customers.

"I'll put enough starch in that you won't be able to bend your arms," he said to one man. And, to a woman, "I treat these shirts like my own children—I slap them around until they're straight and clean." Rosita, too, seemed happy enough. She was usually singing as she worked, some American pop tune but with Korean words dubbed in. She had a soft sweet singing voice. But at night, as if they were werewolves or vampires, their day selves vanished and the fighting began anew.

I had been with Walter for almost two months when I first heard from George. He called one night, sounding much like he used to sound, calm and rational.

"I received your note," George said. Of course he must have received it over a month ago. "About your mother. Her death. I'm sorry," said George.

My mother's funeral had already faded so in my memory that it took a moment for me to respond.

"It's okay," I finally said. "I went to the funeral. I met a half-sister and two half-brothers."

"That must have been nice," George said. "Not the funeral; I mean meeting your sister and brothers."

"It was more strange than nice," I said.

There was a long silence. I could hear George's heavy breath in the phone. I pictured him sitting on our bed in Connecticut. He had folded back the white quilt and propped two pillows beneath his head. He was in a long-sleeved shirt and underwear, his hair still damp from his evening shower, his large feet sticking straight up in the air. The telephone receiver was clutched in his hand as if it were a part of me, my arm or leg, my chin.

"The house is lonely without you," George finally said.

I missed him too and wanted to say so, but could not. "I heard you're back at work," I said instead.

"Yes," George said. "Everyone has been great there. It's as if I never left. I'll be trying my first case next week." Then he said, almost more for himself than for me, "I'm really back to normal, Anne."

"You really sound it," I said and meant it. I wanted to say a lot more. I wanted to tell George about the couple in the laundry downstairs, about their fighting, that they couldn't have a child either. What hatred it brought out in them. I wanted to tell George that my mother died in an accident, that the casket had been kept closed due to her face—it had been destroyed in the crash, and so none of us had really seen her to say good-bye. And I wanted to tell him how often I thought of things we used to do together—reading books to each other out loud, gardening in our backyard, me pulling up tomato plants thinking they were weeds. Driving our old car into the city to visit my father, and once to New Hampshire to visit his mother, singing loudly and out of tune the entire trip. Making love. But all of this, even as I thought it, seemed so far away already, so beside the point.

"We have mice down in the basement," George was

155

saying to me. "I thought I'd buy a cat instead of a trap. Do you want to help pick it out? The cat, I mean."

George had never been good at buying things alone. I helped him shop for all of his clothes, grocery stores left him bewildered, and even on my birthdays and at Christmas he made me tell him not only what I wanted, but the brand, the color, and size.

"Just pick one up at the SPCA," I said.

"Oh sure," George said. He did not sound convinced.

"Buy a gray cat," I added.

"Okay," George said. Then, "I wish you would come home, Anne."

I bit my lip, tried to pretend I was Walter on the phone with a hotline caller. "We both agreed this separation was for the best," I reminded George. "We were making each other miserable."

"You're right," George said. "We were." I heard him shift his weight on the bed and move the receiver to the other hand. I would have reached out and kissed his cheek. I should have done so somehow.

Then we chatted for a few more minutes. He asked about Walter and my father. I asked him more about work and about the house I loved and had left behind. Then we hung up and I felt crueler than Joe downstairs, and as desperate and alone as all those sad people who were right now calling Walter at work.

Although my father is not a particularly sentimental man, he cannot to this day speak of my birth without crying. My birth announcement, yellow and curling, has hung on the kitchen wall of every home he has lived in since I was born.

"You were my first," he has told me as if that was my personal achievement.

"You saved nothing from *my* birth," Walter often complained. "Not a hospital bracelet. Not a lock of hair."

"There is something special about the first," my father always said. "Something entirely magical."

"Thank you," I said.

"It has to do with that feeling of creating life for the first time." Then my father began to weep a little, and I knew he was thinking back on all those years when he and my mother were young and I was the youngest of all.

I never thought I had any great desire for a child; it always was George who spoke of pregnancy, birth. But I knew if I did have one, I would be like my father, sentimental, teary. I once even bought a baby book; it had a quilted cover and pages for when the child first smiled, sat up, took its first step. There were pictures of ducks and teddy bears throughout the book and in the back were blank pages where you could paste your own photographs, your child at one month, six months, its first birthday. I did not show the book to anyone, even George, yet it traveled with me on my move to Connecticut and even back to New York. I thought now it would probably never get filled in. Then I even thought of filling it in with the name and information of a made-up baby. The birth date would be October fourth, the baby would weigh six pounds, six ounces, and would be twenty-one inches long. It would be Alec if it was a boy and Alexandra if it was a girl. Then I took the book out of my suitcase and even filled in both names in front of the book as if the baby were alive, real. Seeing the names written made me cry. Then I giggled because it was so silly to make up an imaginary baby, to actually write about it. So I closed the book, put it away in my suitcase on top of the refrigerator, and listened to Joe and Rosita downstairs.

*   *   *

Walter was off from work one night and he and I were going to a party together. It was being thrown by someone at the radio station where Walter worked and he guaranteed me a good time. As we showered and dressed, Walter first spoke of a particular woman he wanted to know better.

"She has hair so soft you want to sleep on it," Walter told me. "But by sleeping you would miss all the rest of her."

"Quite a dilemma," I said.

At Walter's insistence I had bought a new dress for the party. As I turned in front of the mirror, the tight short cut of the dress, its deep blue color caught me unaware and I thought for a moment I was wearing some other woman's clothing.

Walter whistled. "If you weren't my sister and living here already, I'd take you home with me."

"If you weren't my brother, I would go," I said.

Then Walter began talking about our mother.

"Do you remember watching her get dressed for a party?" he asked.

"Did they go to parties?" I said.

"All the time," said Walter. He slicked his fingers through his short hair, remembered he had forgotten a belt and went back to his room to get one.

"I don't remember," I said. But of course I did have some memories. The black slip of a dress she sometimes wore when she went out in the evenings, the scent of her perfume.

Walter reappeared with his belt. "I always asked her when I'd be old enough to go to the parties with her," Walter said.

"What did she say?" I asked. It was funny that I was not a part of these memories at all; I never watched my mother get dressed, not once.

"She said when I was tall enough to reach her shoulders when we danced," Walter said. "I used to jump onto her bed and tell her I was tall enough. Now."

"Oh Walter," I said.

"Her two sons at the funeral—they were plenty tall enough," said Walter.

Then I thought that our mother had left us before he could barely reach her waist.

The party was downtown in a large loft. Groups of people danced together, their arms around each other's waists; others danced alone. In the corner, a large mirror sat on a table top while guests knelt to do cocaine from its surface. In another corner sat uneaten trays of shrimp, cheeses, assorted tropical fruits. At first I felt strange and lost amid the crowd of new people; I kept looking for Walter and a drink as if I needed one in each hand. Then a man asked me to dance, and then another one. I began to have a good time—the music, the dancing, even the men.

George had never enjoyed dancing.

"I feel big and awkward when I dance," he used to tell me. "And mostly I feel like everyone is going out of their way to step on *my* feet."

"They are big," I used to tease.

George never found that very funny.

George also did not like parties or large groups of people. When we did go to a party he was unfailingly polite, but would station himself in the kitchen or hide in a corner. It was not that he didn't like people, he used to tell me. He just liked them one at a time. I often thought that if George had not liked women and children so much he would have made a good priest. I easily imagined him giving the benediction at mass, his calm voice entrancing the large congregation. The young girls would all whisper and giggle over his large good looks, their mothers would click their tongues—"What a pity *he* would never marry." And the men would admire his rational approach to life. "He's got such a sharp mind for a priest," they might say. After mass George would shake hands, wish his parishioners well. Then he would be alone, quietly going about the rest of his day without any earthly interruptions. Of course, George did not really like to be completely alone. He had told me on the phone he was lonely; I knew it was true.

"What are you thinking about?" my dancing partner asked me. "You have a faraway look to your eyes."

"Must be the drinks," I said.

"They're very pretty eyes," the man said. He took my chin in his hands as if he were about to plant a kiss on my lips. "Very pretty all over," he said.

I blushed and felt needlessly flattered, but when the first song ended, I left the man alone.

Walter was doing flips among the party guests. Chairs and bodies had been cleared away so that Walter could run, jump into the air, and then, after two rolls, tumble to the ground. People clapped, a man hooted, and a woman even did a short cheerleading routine she remembered from high school. Walter was showing off. He bowed after each tumble and kept threatening to do three rolls in the air if there was only enough enthusiasm. The excitement built. The host turned off the stereo and at Walter's request brought two large throw pillows. Someone began to stamp his feet and then others followed. I said nothing.

Walter was preparing to perform the triple roll. He shook his arms and legs like an athlete warming up, he saluted. I ducked into the kitchen to avoid the scene. Walter had done some gymnastics in high school, but he had never been very good. I was embarrassed for him and also fearful of what might happen.

It was just like Walter to do something like this. Similar stunts had been pulled in the past, and though he told me he did it merely to gain attention, I often wondered if there was more to it than that.

The first year after my mother left us, my father was called into Walter's school eight times. Walter was acting up, his teacher told my father. He hid under desks and inside lockers, sent paper airplanes out the window during exams, walked like a duck, made raspberries with his arm. My father would come home from these meetings at the school tired and pale. He would urge Walter to take himself more seriously. Walter giggled.

As if to compensate for Walter's bad behavior, I became rather prissy that first year after my mother left. I cleaned not only my own room, but the entire apartment. I volunteered for extra credit at school, joined clubs, participated in community projects. When my father came home from work I placated him with a drink, and when he brought home his first new woman I welcomed her with open arms. I even took it upon myself to speak with Walter about his behavior.

I led him into my bedroom and we sat down together on my bed.

"Have you seen Dad's face when he comes home from your school?" I said to him. "Every time you're bad he looks more and more unhappy."

"So what," said Walter. I remember he had a pen in his hand and he alternately threw it up in the air as I spoke and wrote on his arm and hand as if he were creating small tatoos.

"You never were this bad when Mom was here," I said to him. "You used to like school."

"I changed my mind," Walter said. He tossed the pen up in the air and missed it on its return. It made a small ink mark on my yellow bedspread.

"Look what you've done!" I said.

Then Walter took the pen and actually began writing on the spread as if my bed were one large sheet of paper.

I felt like shaking him, screaming, but instead I did something much worse. "You're going to drive Dad away too," I said. "Then we'll really be alone."

To this day I regret saying that to Walter. First of all it made him cry, and second of all it wasn't true. I knew Walter had nothing to do with our mother leaving.

"I don't care if he does leave," said Walter, still crying. Then he left the room and it was too late to take the words away.

I suppose we all have our own ways of dealing with loss. Some, like my father, on his fourth wife, lose people so frequently I imagine they begin to hardly notice when someone is gone. For others, certainly for Walter and perhaps for me too, losing someone is like losing a limb. We learn to manage without the arm or leg, learn to compensate, but every time we look down at ourselves, see that gap where our arm or leg should have been, we are newly horrified. A part of us is really gone.

Over the years Walter's behavior did improve, though he continued to pull outrageous stunts among his friends, and at home his humor was often sarcastic, sometimes bitter. At the reception, after my marriage to George, Walter presented us both with a ball and chain, two sets of handcuffs, and an old chastity belt.

"These are the symbols of marriage," said Walter to me and the other assembled guests. "Cherish them. Use them."

I do not remember that either George or I were amused.

"Your brother is something else." It was the man I had danced with, the one who had told me I had pretty

162

eyes. He had discovered my hiding spot in the kitchen. "Did you see him in there doing those flips?" the man said. "Three of them."

"I missed it," I said.

"Well he didn't really get all three of them," the man said. "He hit the floor during the second one. But it was a good try. A damn good try."

The man laughed loudly, then freshened up his drink with a handful of ice and a slosh of scotch. "Your brother must have been doing a lot of toot to pull off a stunt like that."

I frowned at him, and he shrugged.

Sitting down beside me, he fiddled with his glass. "Walter told me you weren't married," he finally said. "But I see you're wearing a wedding band." He picked up my left hand, held it for a moment.

"I'm separated," I said.

"Permanently?" he asked.

I shrugged. George, if he were here, would have told this man to mind his own business. George did not pry into people's lives. He did not gossip. And he believed he should be treated in much the same way.

"I'd like to give you a call sometime, Anne," the man said. I still didn't know his name, but he apparently knew mine. Knew my brother, even. "Could I have your number?" he asked.

"Not tonight," I said. Then, finding my ability to escape this man to be a new and very exhausting experience, I went to retrieve Walter; I was ready to leave the party. Fortunately, after all the tumbling, Walter was rather tired too.

"I bumped my head pretty badly," Walter said in the cab on the ride back to his apartment. He pushed his forehead into my shoulder. "Please rub it, Annie," he said.

I pushed him away. "That's what you get for acting so stupid," I said.

"My fans demanded it," Walter said. He held his head in his hands. "I couldn't let them down."

"What are you trying to prove?" I said. "Who were you trying to impress?"

"Just you, my lovely sister," Walter said. "Just you."

I rolled my eyes, but then smiled. I took Walter's head between my hands and applied pressure to his temples. "Does that feel better?" I said.

"Your hands are magic," said Walter.

From the front seat the cab driver said, "Three eighty-five," and when we didn't move, "You two want to get out."

"She's performing a delicate operation back here," Walter said. "I'm having a baby."

"The meter's running," the cab driver said without smiling.

"I won't name the baby after you," Walter said.

I reached into my purse for the money, fumbling in the dark. When I lifted my head to pay the driver I saw the flames. They were coming out of Walter's apartment building, and there were two fire trucks parked out front. The area was barricaded off, police car lights flashed round and round in the night.

"Walter, your house is on fire," I said.

"Nice try, Annie," he said. Then he saw the fire too.

"Would you mind getting out of the cab," the driver said. "Go help the firemen."

"Fuck off," Walter said, but we exited the cab in a hurry.

The building really was on fire—the laundry downstairs and the few rented apartments upstairs—but it was not as bad as it had first appeared. The firemen had gotten the flames under control. Smoke was heavy in the air and flakes of ash fell down like black snow.

Walter and I pushed our way through the crowd of gapers, right up to the wooden barricades. Walter pushed through those too, and I followed until a police officer in a yellow slicker stopped us.

"Hey you," he said, holding out his arms in front of us. "Where do you think you're going?"

"I live here," Walter said. He pointed with his finger so that he just narrowly missed the policeman's ear.

"Me too," I said.

"Not anymore," the policeman said.

"What do you mean?" Walter said.

"I mean the entire building is closed down and will be for the duration," the officer said.

"All my stuff is in there," Walter said.

He was practically screaming now, and, trying to help, I interrupted as politely as I could.

"What exactly happened?" I asked.

"A fire, Annie," said Walter. "What do you think happened."

I did not look at Walter, but at the police officer. I asked *him* how the fire had started.

"It started in the laundry," he said. "The Asian lady set the place on fire. Poured gasoline over a pile of dirty shirts. Lit a match. And boom."

"Really," I said. I tried to imagine Rosita starting a fire. Was it during a fight with Joe, or were they already in bed? Had she lain awake, plotting, waiting, preparing to perform the arson, to kill him?

"The Chinese lady just lost it," the officer said. "Go figure."

Walter did not look impressed. After all, it was his apartment.

"We already got the lady's statement," the policeman continued. "It seems she was trying to kill her husband, and herself too. Go figure."

"I'd like to," said Walter.

"Was anybody hurt?" I asked.

The flames had completely died down now and the crowd was slowly dispersing. Smoke choked the air. The building looked black and skeletal.

"Her legs were burned pretty badly—we sent her to the hospital. The mental hospital, if you ask me. Her husband escaped without a scratch. I don't know how."

"What about upstairs?" I asked.

"The firemen got everyone out from there," the policeman said. "Nothing too dramatic, but you two were lucky to be away tonight." Then he continued to talk about the fire, about Rosita and Joe, about the filed report down at the station.

"Hey, you all did a fine job," Walter interrupted. "But what about my apartment, my stuff?"

"Nothing left," the policeman said. "Go figure."

I took Walter by the arm and led him away. There was really nothing to be done tonight.

"I'm going to miss my record albums," Walter said to me. "I had every Beatle album produced in the U.S."

"I'm sorry," I said. We stood back on the opposite side of the street and watched the firemen finish the job. They doused the building with water, others entered downstairs with equipment I could not identify. One truck even left the scene.

"Some letters," Walter continued, and then, as if just remembering a fond friend, "My favorite pair of jeans."

I had lost only some clothing, and my baby book. But it wasn't as if there was actually a baby.

166

"At least we weren't inside when it happened," I said. "At least we're alive." I was thinking of myself up there, alone most nights, going to bed early, waking up to the smell of smoke, intense heat.

"I know," Walter said. Then he sighed loudly, and like a little boy said, "Dammit. All my shirts were in the laundry, too."

I looked at the building, thought of Rosita's charred legs, shook my head. "Everything is replaceable," I said to Walter.

Without warning, Walter took hold of my arm and gave it a sharp twist. "Don't you say that," he said. Then, letting go, he looked at me as if the skin on my face had just fallen off.

"You sound just like Mom and Dad when you talk like that," he said. His voice was angry, hurt. He pulled me around so our foreheads were nearly touching. "Whether you know it or not, Annie," he said, "some things are not replaceable."

"Okay," I said, pulling away.

"I mean it," Walter said.

I knew he did and I knew he was right. But then, some people do not want what they've lost replaced. Like Rosita, they would rather be rid of it all—the laundry, her husband Joe, even herself.

"Let's go get a drink," said Walter finally.

I agreed, but, although we passed many open restaurants and bars, we did not go in. Instead we kept walking. Round and round the block, looking at the black, gutted laundry, weighing the damage, the cost.

THE BEAUTY
OF THE PLAN

My father told us we were a family that rallied together in times of need. That is what he always taught us, and that is what we practiced when needs arose.

"Fortunately those times are rare indeed," my father used to add. "It would be rather tedious to be bailing you kids out all the time."

But of course, that was exactly what my father did. When Walter was young and ran away from home, my father drove 150 miles to retrieve him. When I broke my leg at sixteen my father made certain that I was chauffeured about to school, on dates, to the junior prom. In college, my father sent us money and airplane tickets, and flew up to see us when we were feeling down or needed encouragement during exams. Perhaps he felt he had to compensate for our lack of a mother, or perhaps my father actually liked feeling needed so much. At any rate, even in adulthood he has been there for Walter and me, watching us each fail in various relationships, squander our inheritances. And when Walter's apartment burned down, I certainly expected that, once again, we would be calling on my father for his help.

At least for a while, I was wrong. After the fire I learned something about my brother that truly amazed me. Walter owned and was now collecting on a personal insurance policy.

"Insurance?" I said to him. He had shown me the check, told me it was to cover his damages and loss—the stacks of record albums, the king-sized mattress, his clothes. And this loss was significant, Walter informed me, sounding just as he must have sounded when he spoke to the claims department at Liberty Home Mutual. My brother sounded like an adult.

"But, insurance," I said. "Of all people, you are the one I least expected to own an insurance policy. To even think about insurance."

Walter spoke to me quite seriously. "Look, Annie," he said. "I may be a fuckup, but I'm not stupid. I've got to protect my interests. A fire or flood can ruin you, wipe you out. Certainly you've heard the ads."

"A flood?" I said. "In New York?"

"From sewer overload," said Walter.

I shook my head. "I thought I knew you," I said to my brother. "It was something I could count on." I took the insurance check from him, brushed my fingers across its embossed numbers, and even checked the signature to assure myself of its authenticity. It was very real. $3,500 to compensate for loss. "I don't know you at all," I said.

Walter put his arm around my waist as if I were a

child that needed comforting, and squeezed me tight. At least he still felt the same. "Don't worry, Annie," he said, and he nuzzled my neck. He even smelled the same. "I'm sure I'll do something right in character any moment. I'll restore your faith in no time."

Of course he was right. Although our father advised Walter to use the money to replace the essentials he had lost in the fire, and then put the remaining amount in a short term CD or money market account, that was not to be. Instead, Walter cashed the entire check and one week later presented the money to me on the floor of my father's vast living room. The money was entirely in small bills.

"What is all this?" I said. I had just returned from work at the bookstore, and in the bitter winter frost I had taken two subways and walked four considerably long blocks to get to my father's home. Walter and I were both living there now, just as if we were still young children, and although I had my own room, and even a closet to hold my clothing, I sensed this arrangement was to be even more temporary than the ill-fated apartment I had shared with Walter. That had lasted not even four months.

It was not that my father intimated that we should grow up or even leave. In fact, the opposite was true. Isabelle and her children were in Europe for the winter visiting her family, and my father, who had stayed behind to work, enjoyed having his own children home once again. He encouraged us to remain as long as we liked, and although my father is prone to exaggeration, we took him at his word.

We acted as if we had never grown up, never gone to college, never gotten married, never moved away. Once back in my father's home I allowed the maid to prepare my meals, clean up after me, even make my bed. I

quarreled often with Walter, squabbles over the bathroom, the television, or a particular section in the
newspaper. And I also did not see any men. I like to think
it was because I was being faithful to George; although
separated, we were certainly not divorced. No legal pro-
ceedings had been discussed. But I did not date because
living back in my father's home I merely felt too young.

The piles of money on the living room floor were
considerable. Walter had sorted the bills into ones, fives,
tens, and twenties, neat and crisp.

"What is all this?" I said again, but I already knew
from the grin on Walter's face that this was his insurance
reward.

"Let's do something reckless, Annie," Walter said,
and he waltzed me into the room, pulling off my coat and
gloves as we circled the money. "Let's be reckless," he
said.

"Walter," I said, but I allowed him to lead me to the
floor.

"This is our ticket out of here," Walter said, very
dramatically. He picked up one of the piles and rocked it
like a baby. Then, as if the money were the snow collecting on the balcony ledge outside, he rolled a pile into a
green paper snowball and tossed it into my face.

"Isn't this fun?" said Walter.

"You bet," I said. I pulled off my boots, then my
stockings, and stretched my legs across the warm carpet.
Except for Walter, the large apartment was hushed, silent.
My father was still at work. The maid was in the kitchen
resting before dinner. Only Walter and I were witness to
the seduction of this warm room on a winter day, of all
this money.

"Let's be free, Annie, love," said Walter. "Just hear
my plan." And, sitting comfortably next to a pile of tens
that rose to my kneecaps, I listened.

171

The plan was to go camping in Canada. We would be gone for at least three weeks, possibly more. We would rent a car with snow tires and a ski rack. And Walter would purchase all the equipment—the down sleeping bags, the expedition-quality tent—and would take care of all expenses. This was his and Liberty Home Mutual's treat.

"Camping in the winter?" I said. "Won't we freeze?"

"We'll keep each other warm," said Walter.

"But what do we know about camping, anyway?" I said.

"There's actually not too much to know," Walter said. "That's the beauty of the plan."

"Oh, is that the beauty," I said.

"Live a little, Annie," Walter said.

But I really wasn't sure that I could.

Whenever George and I had traveled together, gone on vacation, taken a trip, our itinerary was always carefully planned.

George would research our destination in books, underlining and highlighting, making notations on places of interest, the best restaurants, the cleanest hotels. All reservations were made in advance. Just as thoroughly, I would make lists of items needed to be packed, I plotted the entire contents of our luggage, and then I mapped our course. And, whether it was by car or plane or bus, I knew the exact time of departure and arrival, rest areas, meals served. We were always well prepared.

"You travel like an old lady," Walter said.

"I travel cautiously," I answered.

Travel with Walter would be chaotic. We would arrive in towns whose names I could not pronounce, hike to where there were no phones or mail delivery, sleep far from what I could remember or even know. And oh, how enticing it was, for there was much I wanted to leave behind.

George had been calling me, asking me to please come back home.

"I've changed," he said. I believed he might have. "I love you," he said, and though I loved him too, merely the thought of our house in Connecticut left me fearful and chilled.

I would have liked to have left behind my job at the bookstore as well; the novelty of being among the books again had worn off, the pay was low. And my father's apartment, too, with its pristine white walls, its soft, soft carpeting, made me unhappy, somehow did not feel like home.

Even so, I could not leave. I rationalized my decision. If I were only younger, I told Walter, I would go. If I were only single.

"Bullshit," Walter said. "Like hell you would have gone."

He was right. Even when I was young and single, even as a child, I had never been reckless. Rather, hopelessly responsible, as if some large bell were hanging on the wall above me, prepared to chime if I were late or even so slightly strayed.

So Walter went on his camping trip alone. Before he left, my father gave Walter an American Express card.

"If you get into trouble, you use this," he told Walter.

"Dad," Walter said, putting the card back into my father's hand. "I've got cash."

"That's not accepted everywhere, you know," my father said.

"I'll face that inconvenience," Walter said very bravely, but he took the card back nonetheless.

Then Walter took me aside and kissed me once, and then again.

"Make sure your life doesn't stop while I'm gone, Annie," he said.

"I do fine without you," I said.

"You have a tendency to check out of life for a while," Walter said.

"Look who's leaving," I said.

But we both knew what Walter had meant.

After he was gone, my life, the routine of my days, did not change so very much. For the first couple of days, commuting back and forth to work, I had a few regrets, but then they were gone. And during the first week of Walter's trip, my father and I spent quite a bit of time worrying about Walter's survival. We sat at home nights, listening to the weather reports from Canada and reading books on winter camping. We asked each other if Walter had brought along a down parka, if he had plenty of freeze-dried food, waterproof boots. When he called, which was infrequent, we clung to the telephone long after he had hung up, as if that would somehow keep him safe from harm.

By the end of the week, however, we had already followed Walter's passage up to the Gaspé Peninsula in Quebec, and our grip on Walter relaxed, our fears subsided. I went out a few nights with some old friends and when I returned I found my father had actually missed the weather on TV. I returned all the camping books to the shelves where I worked. We forgot where Walter had said he might travel next.

Walter had been gone for over two weeks when George called to ask me out on a date.

"Just a date," George assured me. "Dinner, some drinks."

Although I am usually a quick liar and have had much practice, I could think of no excuse to tell George. I accepted his invitation; I said yes.

George took me to a restaurant we used to frequent while we were dating. It was a small quiet place and although the food was not exceptional, it was served with such charm and grace that we always overlooked the flaws.

The waiter remembered us and brought us our favorite bottle of wine and some Italian bread.

"I haven't seen you two in such a long while," the waiter said.

"We've been busy," I said.

"One should never be too busy for food or love," he said and then disappeared.

"I'm not too busy," George said, and when he took my hand I let him kiss each one of my fingers. The familiar is always so alluring when it suddenly seems new.

Over veal and mushrooms, we talked about our house in Connecticut. George had refinished all the wood floors downstairs, had repainted the kitchen, and had installed all new storm windows.

"I've always enjoyed that kind of work," said George.

"I know," I said.

Then I told George about Walter's trip.

"He rented a VW Rabbit, packed it up, and took off," I said. "Already he has hiked two small mountains in Canada."

"He went alone?" George said.

"He wanted me to go with him," I said.

"You would never have gone," George said, and I shrugged.

While we ate our dessert of pear tarts and cream, George told me I looked different.

175

"I'm wearing my hair in a new way," I said, fingering my short blond hair. I had always worn it long, and cutting it had seemed as serious as cosmetic surgery.

"Well, yes," George said. "But something else, too."

"I'm older," I said.

"Maybe that's it," said George.

After dinner we took a short walk. The night air was so cold it stung my cheeks and all our talk was accented by the steam rising from our lips. We passed our old apartment, its windows lit up, and George patted its brick wall hello. Then we hailed a cab and I directed the driver to take us to my father's apartment uptown.

Inside, I could hear the purr of the television from the maid's room, but the rest of the apartment was quiet, empty. My father was out for the evening. George and I were alone.

I had been using my father's study as a bedroom. His desk and papers had been pushed against one wall. A bookshelf had been partially cleared for some of my belongings. The room was dark and smelled of old paper and ink, a subtle and comforting smell.

"Is this your room now?" George said.

"Not much," I said.

Still, the couch opened out into a queen-sized bed, and that is where George and I made love. It had been so many months that we were like two teenagers together for the first time. Nervous, unsure of what we were doing, but eager and very easy to please. We were serious, and when it was over George kissed me more gently than I have ever been kissed. Like a soap bubble landing on a crystal vase; that is how I thought of the kiss later, after he was gone.

"Come home with me, Anne," George said, and he was warm around me. "I know I can make you happy."

"I don't know," I said, now much more by rote than actual conviction.

"It can work this time," said George.

I wanted to believe him, but it was too easy to remember George in the hospital watching TV, George abandoning me after his father's funeral, or even George sitting across the table from me over countless dinners, reading the paper, not talking, somewhere else.

"Maybe it just wasn't supposed to last forever," I said. "Maybe we were meant to go our separate ways."

"Marriage isn't like that," George said.

"I don't know," I said, and I got out of the bed, pulled on my robe, and left the room. I sat in the kitchen of my father's apartment in the dark for over an hour, and when I returned to the study, George was gone.

The next morning at 5:05 I was awakened by the telephone. I imagined before I answered that it might be George and I thought quickly how I would respond—distant and nearly ignorant of what had gone on between us last night. I could always plead too much to drink. However, it was not George, and although I reached the phone before my father or the maid, they both joined me in the kitchen, not yet dressed and half-asleep, to hear the disturbing news.

It was a hospital just outside of Augusta, Maine. Walter was there in the intensive care unit hooked up to a respirator and I.V., his legs crushed beneath him. They got our name, the hospital told me, from my father's American Express card.

"What happened?" I said, and although I thought I was shouting my voice was barely a whisper.

He had been in a car accident, the administrator from the hospital told me. Walter's car had skidded into a snowplow coming toward him in the other lane. It was snowing hard, the roads were slick. The rental car had folded like a piece of aluminum foil. And there had been a girl with him, too, the hospital informed me. Did I know who she was, and when I said no, they told me she was dead.

I am excitable by nature; rain on a day scheduled for a picnic, a train running late, even a spilled and broken glass can cause me to panic or cry. But faced with real emergency, honest pain, I am suddenly calm, almost relaxed. So it was that morning. I diligently got paper and pen and was patient with the hospital as I wrote down the address, directions, my brother's room number. When I hung up my voice was soft as I told my father and the maid what had occurred. Later I called my boss at work, told her I would not be in, and then I went to pack my bags. And throughout the drive to the airport, the shuttle to Boston, and then the short flight to Augusta, I soothed my father, bought him a drink and headphones, and told him over and over that Walter would be fine.

"You know our family," I said to my father more than once. "We always survive."

Walter was small, like a child, in the hospital bed, and pale like the underside of an unripened piece of fruit. There was an I.V. bottle hanging above him, purplish rings around his eyes, a tube through his nose, and although his legs were covered up I could see the bulk of the bandages and casts. Even so, I expected one of Walter's comments, jokes. "See what you missed, Annie," I thought he might say. "See what excitement you gave up." But Walter said nothing when we arrived. He did not even smile.

"Walter," I said. "It's me—Anne."

He only nodded and then closed his eyes, and it wasn't until later when my father sat beside him, brushed his fingers over Walter's newly grown beard, that Walter took my father's hand, and they sat that way throughout the night, eyeing each other, thinking of the past.

We spent our days at the hospital and our nights in two adjoining hotel rooms a block away. Walter's recovery was slow; his legs, encased in two plaster casts, were not healing properly. And even after the respirator was removed, Walter said very little. The doctor spoke of extended care, and once even of amputation.

"His right leg is badly infected," the doctor said. "It may need to be removed." And our horror at this news was such that the doctor turned and walked away.

In the evenings my father called Isabelle in France. I am sure the telephone bills were astronomical, but whatever solace she offered him seemed to help. My father joined me after these calls, and he seemed stronger, his face almost human.

I spoke to no one, did not talk to friends or George. But on our fifth day at the hospital I finally met the parents of the girl who had been with Walter in the crash. The girl who had not lived.

Her parents had come in to see Walter. I believe they had chosen the time deliberately; it was when my father and I usually left the room to eat dinner down in the hospital cafeteria. However, this evening I had sensed some improvement in Walter's condition and I sent my father on alone.

The girl's name was Roxanne Flint. She was a local girl and Walter had met her at the diner where she worked. They spent time together after her shift, and such was the attraction that she even brought him to her home one evening to meet her family.

I met the Flints just outside Walter's room; they were peering through the door as if to determine how injured Walter really was. I could see from the look on the father's face that this was not to be a friendly visit.

Walter had been trying to convince Roxanne to go with him on his travels, her parents told me, to quit her job and see some of the world. She had never been outside of Maine in her life.

"We of course disapproved of the idea," her mother said. "She barely knew him."

"We did not like your brother," said Mr. Flint.

"I'm sorry," I said. "I'm so sorry about everything."

I kept the couple out in the hall; I did not want Walter to see them, hear them, and I did not want them near him, either. Huddled together, we stood underneath the fluorescent lights, leaning against the stark walls, and talked for quite some time.

"She was only twenty-two," Mrs. Flint told me. "And she was so badly crushed they would not even let us see her. Our only daughter."

"Your brother killed her," Mr. Flint said. He was a large man, and when he said this he looked down, dwarfing me and his wife. "He killed our Roxanne."

I tried to tell them there had been no alcohol or drugs involved, no reckless driving. It had been an icy and narrow road, a dark night. But they could not be convinced and I am not sure I blamed them. If it had been Roxanne driving, my brother killed, there would be no consolation, no point of understanding. I would want someone to blame.

They spoke some more about their only daughter; she had been saving up for a car, she had been a prom queen in high school, she knew how to make paper flowers, she had red hair.

180

"When she was little I used to braid her hair," her mother told me. "She always wore it long."

Then they left, both of them, without seeing Walter, and in tears. Just before they reached the end of the hall, however, Mr. Flint turned and walked back toward me.

"I just want to tell your brother what he did," the man said. "I want him to know."

But I would not let him in the room, and finally the wife took her husband's arm and led him quickly away.

"That was Roxanne's parents," Walter said in a weak voice when I joined him back in the room. A nurse had shaved off his beard that morning, and when he raised the head of his bed to see me his face looked as it had when he was thirteen. I wanted him to be thirteen again. I would be fourteen, and we would taunt each other like children, say mean things, for we had no fears then, at least for each other, of separation or loss.

"That was them," I said to Walter. Then I sat next to him on the narrow hospital bed, looked at the watercolor hanging on the wall; it was a beach scene but did not remind me of any beach I had ever known.

"I guess she died," Walter said, and a short while later, "I knew she died." Then he cried, the first time since we had come up to be with him, heaving as if in great pain. Walter's crying did not last long, though, and after I called the nurse for some juice, Walter went to sleep and did not speak of Roxanne again. Still I believe, however little mourning he may have done for Roxanne, it was enough. Having someone to grieve for other than himself changed the course of my brother's recovery, and he slowly began to come back to us.

Weeks later we finally returned to New York. My father furnished the guest room with a hospital bed and wheelchair and hired a full-time nurse to help my brother relearn how to walk. Although Walter's right leg had not been amputated, the cast on it would remain for over six months, and he would forever walk with a limp, use a cane.

"Mr. Gimp, to you," Walter introduced himself to the nurse when they met. She did not smile, but I did. It was good to be home again.

In the bookstore I worked with renewed vigor and was promoted for my efforts with a position as a full-time salesperson. I recommended books for children, books for people with hobbies, books for those who were ill.

After work and on weekends, I spent time with Walter. Spring had arrived in the city and I took Walter to the park, past the stores that stretched up Fifth Avenue, and once, when he felt particularly strong, to the zoo.

Although self-conscious of his wheelchair, Walter enjoyed the animals, and even the children.

"I guess they're all wondering why a young guy like me is sitting in this chair," he said to me outside the monkey house. It was true the children stared at him when we passed.

"They probably imagine it's a sports injury," I said.

"That's not what that chimpanzee is thinking," Walter said, pointing to an ape standing in front, peering through the bars of its cage. "He's thinking cripple, but is too polite to say so."

I rolled my eyes and Walter laughed. Then I laughed, too, and we stopped thinking for a moment that Walter needed to be wheeled around, that he needed help to the bathroom, to get dressed in the morning, to take a bath.

Further on we saw the wildcats and the bears, and we spent a long time in front of the elephants; as children we had always liked the elephants best. I bought some peanuts out of the vending machine and we let the elephants pick them up one by one from the palms of our hands.

There were parents with children there, too, and at one point Walter pointed to a small girl and smiled. "That girl looks just like you," he said, nudging me in her direction. The girl, who was probably just four years old, had long, straight hair and blue eyes. She was dressed in a red skirt and black tights, and she very properly held onto her father's arm, sniffed silently at the other children who screamed when the elephants' long trunks stretched toward them over the iron bars.

"She even acts like you," Walter said.

"Really," I said, and as I looked at the girl, watched her and her father finally walk away, I felt the first tug of something strange in my body. Like the beginnings of the flu when you're feeling achy and sore, but before the really miserable phase of being sick is upon you. I thought I might be pregnant.

I told no one, but that night after dinner I went to the pharmacy and purchased a home pregnancy test kit. I locked the bathroom door and followed the instructions carefully, holding the vial steady so that its contents would not be disturbed, and when the test proved positive I poured the blue liquid down the toilet and flushed it away.

I knew the baby was George's; he had been the only one in months. We had proven the doctors and tests wrong and together had created a new life. If George and I had still been together, I would have broken the news to him shyly, as if revealing some deep secret, and he would have blushed, would have held me in his arms. And later, after we had fully accepted the fact of the baby, the miracle, George would have told me that nothing had ever made him so happy in his life.

But George was in Connecticut, and I was sitting on the floor of my father's bathroom tracing my fingers over the white tiles, wondering about being pregnant, the changes I could expect to occur in my body, trying not to think about the baby at all.

It wasn't until a week later that I revealed my secret. I had offered to take Walter to the hospital to have his legs checked, one cast removed, the other changed. He would be getting a walking cast on his right leg, and although I had been advised differently, I had hopes of Walter walking home beside me. I gave his nurse the afternoon off, called in sick to work, and with the doorman's help managed to get Walter and his wheelchair into a cab.

I sat with Walter in the waiting room, looking with him through an issue of *People* magazine. But once he had been taken in to see the doctor, I left and rode the elevator to the third floor to my own doctor's office. There, among the tweedy chairs and talc-colored carpeting, I collected all their literature on pregnancy and scheduled an appointment for what would be the first of many prenatal exams. The nurse assured me that, if done correctly, the home tests were accurate. Then she congratulated me and smiled, and my doctor kissed me on the cheek.

"So you did this without our help," he said to me. Over a year ago, when George and I were still trying to get pregnant, this same doctor had recommended some tests, a specialist for George, and even fertility drugs, but we had disregarded his advice. "I'm very happy for you," the doctor said.

"I'm happy too," I said, but I still was not sure that I was.

Then I left the office, rode the elevator back down, and went to retrieve my brother.

They were just wheeling Walter out when I arrived. I was disappointed to see he looked not so very different from before. Although his left leg was no longer in a cast, it looked thin and hairless, and it was covered with a yellow waxy coating. His right leg was in a smaller cast, but it too did not seem capable of carrying even half of my brother's weight.

"I thought he would be walking," I whispered to the doctor.

"Not for a long time, if ever," the doctor whispered back.

"Just wait," I hissed. "I make it a habit of proving doctors wrong."

"However," the doctor said, and he patted me on the back, "they are not *your* legs."

Walter looked sad on the ride home; although he did not say so, I could tell he was discouraged as well. He kept looking at the leg that was not in the cast, feeling it below his shortened pant leg.

"It feels inhuman," Walter said. "It feels like something you wouldn't want to touch."

That was when I decided to tell him about the baby.

"Guess what?" I said.

"That's what," said Walter.

"No, really," I said.

"What is it, Annie?" he said. His voice was dry, impatient.

Then I sprang it on him. "I'm pregnant," I said. "I'm going to have a baby."

"Is this a joke?" Walter said.

"No," I said. "The test tube turned blue."

Walter looked at me strangely. Then he asked if it was George's, and when I nodded yes, he grinned and hugged me so tight I gasped and coughed.

"Hey," I said.

"You two do things in strange ways," Walter said, still hugging me. "You separate, and *then* you have the baby. Long-distance copulation. But," and Walter shrugged, "whatever works."

"It's hard to believe," I said.

"That you two could actually pull it off," Walter said, and then, "A baby. Wow."

"I wasn't sure you could be happy," I said. "You never liked George."

"But a baby," said Walter.

"Wow," I said.

Then we giggled, like children, all the way home.

That night I lay awake in bed for a long time. As my eyes adjusted to the darkness, I began to read the titles of my father's books sitting on the shelves. When I grew bored with that, I began to read the names of each of the authors.

"Balzac," I read. "Charles Dickens, E. M. Forster, Thomas Hardy." Thomas would make a nice boy's name, I thought. We would call him Tom.

Then I began to think about the baby. It was probably no larger than a pea right now, hardly a baby at all. It would be months yet, and an entirely different season, before it was born. And then, where would I keep it? There was no room for a crib in my father's study, much less all the other paraphernalia one collects after a baby is born. I couldn't very well store it all in a box under the bed. And wouldn't Isabelle object to all of us in the apartment—Walter and his nurse, me and the baby?

"This isn't a rooming house, you know," Isabelle would say to me, though not unkindly. "I have my own children to think about, and I don't even let *them* stay here all the time." Isabelle was so right.

I could go back to Connecticut, I thought. George wanted me back and there would be plenty of room for the baby there. I imagined setting up a nursery in the small bedroom upstairs, the one that got the early morning sun. George would paint a caravan of animals along the ceiling and I would hang a mobile above the crib, sing nursery rhymes before bed. A baby could be happy in a room like that.

But I wasn't sure that I could be happy in a house like that, living with George. Our marriage, even at the beginning, so filled with plans, had never been what we had always hoped, and even assumed, our marriage would be like. I loved him, of course, but that had failed us, and did I now suppose a baby could make a difference, could alter what we could not?

I turned over on my stomach in bed. Soon I would not be able to do that, but for now I could not feel the baby inside me. I imagined it was like a small pink marble, round and rolling, searching for a comfortable spot to settle down and grow. It kept rolling, though, and I followed it in my mind, up and around and back down, as the night crept slowly toward morning.

The next day at breakfast, Walter hit me with an ultimatum. Everyone was there—my father, Isabelle and Gregory back from France, even Walter's nurse. It was Saturday and Isabelle had prepared a large breakfast of omelets and smoked fish, bowls filled with freshly cut strawberries and melon.

Walter sat in the chair next to me with his right leg propped up on a second chair. He nearly shouted in my ear.

"Annie," he said. "I've been thinking all night about what you told me yesterday."

"What did she tell you?" my father asked.

Isabelle cut up some fish and placed it in front of Gregory; she looked at me, raised her eyebrows, said nothing.

"And I've concluded," Walter continued, "that you must return to George. You must keep your family intact."

"What is all this about?" my father said, tapping loudly on his glass with his spoon. "What are you talking about?"

"Must we have quite this much racket, first thing in the morning?" Isabelle said.

"I like racket," said Gregory.

"You must go back to George," Walter said again; his voice was not teasing, but insistent, like my father's voice, and demanding. "He is your husband," Walter said. "You are married."

"Her husband is crazy," Isabelle said. "Insane." She frowned at Walter, then carefully poured my father a cup of coffee, adding just a touch of cream. "And I don't believe they're really married anymore."

"They are," Walter said.

"In this family, unless I say otherwise, we make our own choices," my father said. "This is Annie's choice. George is *her* husband."

"George is also the father of *her* child," said Walter.

I thought the room collectively gasped, and then there was silence, disturbed only by the sound of Gregory hitting his foot against the leg of his chair. Isabelle handed my father his cup of coffee. Everyone looked at me.

And though I had said nothing during all of this, I finally spoke up. "Yes, I am pregnant," I said. Despite myself, I smiled. "I'm going to have a baby."

"With George?" Isabelle said.

"I don't want a baby," Gregory said.

"A baby," my father said, and he touched my cheek as if he were seeing me for the first time.

When the excitement died down, when everyone finished kissing me, when all had touched my still-flat stomach, asked to hear the story of me and George and our evening out again and again, when breakfast was finally over, Walter and I went into my father's study to be alone.

There had been many talks in this room over the years, or ones just like it in all the many houses and apartments in our childhood. Walter picked up a paperweight from my father's desk and tossed it up in the air, caught it, and did this over and over again. I looked at the floor, at my shoes, refolded the cuff of my shirt. My father, who had always led these kinds of talks in the past, was not here with us; Walter and I had to do this ourselves.

"I don't understand you," I said finally to Walter. "You always encouraged me to leave George. You didn't like him. You didn't think we were good for each other."

Walter dropped the paperweight, and I had to pick it up for him. He nodded. "I've changed my mind," said Walter.

"You can't do that," I said. "Not now."

Walter ignored me. "We can't keep disposing of each other," he said. "In this family, when we get tired of someone, when we grow bored, when someone just doesn't look new anymore, we throw them away." Then he looked down at his own legs as if he would have liked to throw them away, trade them in for a new pair; I'm sure he would have, if given the chance. "People are not like trash," Walter said.

I shook my head. "I don't understand you," I said.

"Yes you do," said Walter.

He maneuvered his wheelchair around the cluttered

room until he was right next to me. He took my hand. His touch made me think of another time, years back, before I married George, when Walter had taken my hand and we had danced together in a bar near the beach. People had looked at us, not knowing we were brother and sister, and imagined we were in love, but later when we changed partners we looked at someone new with those same eyes.

"You really want me to go back to George?" I said.

"I really do," Walter said. Then, after we had sat together a little longer, he said, "Annie, it is going to be an amazing baby."

"You bet," I said.

"And it deserves a real home," Walter said. "And real parents."

"I know," I said, and I did.

Then Walter turned his chair around to face the bookshelves behind him and reached for my father's large book of Bartlett's quotations; it was up high and I had to help Walter get it down, placed it on his lap. Then we read from it for almost an hour—all the passages on children and family, on homes and even on marriage. We believed it was what our father would have done.

AFTER THE DREAM

"In my dream," I told my family, "The baby was already born."

"Was it healthy?" George asked.

"Was it a boy?" my father asked. "Or a girl?"

But in my dream the baby was neither boy nor girl, nor even human. The baby was a small gray kitten, and I carried it at my breast, stroking its soft velvety ears.

"Your baby was a cat?" Walter said. "Great, Annie. Just great."

"I loved it like a baby," I told them. And I remembered in the dream that when I pressed the kitten close to nurse I felt not skin, but fur and its cold pink nose. When it opened its mouth to cry it made a small meow, and I felt it was a helpless sound, but nonetheless strong, demanding.

"In my dream, of course," I told my family, "you were all delighted. You spoke of the kitten's beauty, of its intelligent face, its attentive eyes."

"Of course we were delighted," my father said. "It was our grandchild."

But it isn't human, I told them all in my dream. My face flushed, my neck was warm. It's a kitten, can't you see! And I held the animal up so that they could see.

George took my hand and looked at me strangely. "Was I there?" he said. "In the dream?"

I nodded, and then I remembered the rest of the dream, so terrifying still, I shuddered.

"Then I lost it," I told my family. "I lost the kitten."

Startled, George let go of my hand and looked at me as if I *had* actually lost something, though perhaps nothing as valuable as a real baby.

"You lost it?" George said. "You lost the baby."

"It was a kitten," I insisted.

"A kitten or a baby," my father said. "What was the difference, really."

I remembered in the dream I had put the kitten outside in the backyard on the grass. It was a warm autumn day, but still I had covered it with a quilt we used to keep in the beach house. Then I had gone inside to answer the telephone. I would be gone just a minute, I told the kitten. Don't be frightened. I left it there purring in the grass. And when I returned the kitten was gone.

"I searched everywhere," I told my family. "I pleaded for help. But all anyone could say was it's only a kitten. Don't worry, Annie, it's only a kitten." Then I woke up.

Isabelle came up and touched my cheek. "I had strange dreams like that when I was pregnant, too," she said. "As the pregnancy progressed, the dreams got stranger."

"I think it sounds crazy," Walter said. "Thinking your baby would look like a kitten."

"It *was* a kitten," I said.

"Anne's not crazy," my father said. "That's the last thing Annie is."

George looked down at the sand and at his bare feet; he was still sensitive about the word "crazy." When he finally looked up, he said, "I think it was the baby's dream, not yours."

"The baby's dream?" I said. "Do they actually dream in the womb?"

"I know our baby does," George said.

Then we all fell silent, thinking of the baby sleeping inside my stomach, inside the womb, dreaming its horribly frightening dreams all alone.

We were, all of us, the entire family, at the beach house for the whole month of August. We had not spent a summer vacation together in years, and when we first arrived at the house, en masse in a caravan of three cars, everything seemed too quiet and fragile to touch. Although the maids had been in, the furniture was covered with a fine layer of dust, the blinds were drawn, and the two front hall lights were out. As we stood there inside the doorway, looking at one another, all the memories of summers past seemed hidden in that small darkness, ready to appear when the light bulbs were finally changed.

Of course there were many of us and we filled the quiet house quickly. Isabelle and my father, and Yvette and Gregory. Walter, in a walking cast and cane, was there without his nurse. And then there was George and me. I was over seven months pregnant that August, so there was the presence of *that* baby too.

Because of the past, I think, or maybe just because it

was summer, we all spent as little time as possible in the house, but instead gathered out on the beach. Walter had difficulty walking with his cane on the sand, so he and I often sat together on the large beach blanket under the umbrella to protect ourselves from the hot sun. The rest of the family spent their days in the water, swimming or bobbing on rubber rafts in the waves.

I had tried swimming. My doctor and even Isabelle had recommended it during pregnancy for the feeling of weightlessness, buoyancy. But it was not for me. In the water I felt the baby push against my lungs and other organs, constricting, pressing, fighting for the space inside my body I had once considered mine alone. I found myself gasping for breath, bending over with cramps, and I would struggle out of the water to be free.

At mealtimes and sometimes even more frequently, the rest of the family would join Walter and me on our blanket in the sand.

"Miss us?" they would say, their suits dripping onto our dry legs, their wet hair plastered to their scalps.

"Not really," Walter always replied, but he made room for them just the same.

We would all sit together, then, sharing sandwiches and fruit, sipping lemonade, and we would talk to one another, not cautiously, but not quite as openly as in the years before. In the summers I remembered from child-hood, there had never been taboo subjects, so many words unspoken, and now there were.

After I told my family about the dream, George left us and went back up to the house for a nap, and my father sat down in the empty space beside me.

"This is the first summer since you were a baby that I can't see your ribs," my father said to me softly.

"Skinny Annie finally fills out a little," said Walter.

"Don't embarrass her," Isabelle said, and I blushed all the more.

In my black maternity swimsuit my stomach stuck out, not like a grapefruit or a watermelon as I've sometimes heard it described, but like a baby. Odd, irregularly shaped, not too large, but certainly not small. And every so often I would feel the baby shift its weight, move from front to back, or stick its leg out to stretch, and the shape of my stomach would alter. Hardening here, softening there. Just like a baby.

I think it was this baby, in fact, that had brought us all together once more. Since George was the father, his past misdeeds were forgiven, and in my family he had finally obtained certain territorial rights. He spoke more, played a more aggressive game of touch football on the beach, and he stated his requests for dinner just like the rest of us. He did not venture to tell a joke, but George had never been a joke teller. However, before dinner one night he did open a bottle of wine, and after pouring us each a glass he actually made a toast.

"To the baby," George said.

"Is that it?" said my father.

"That's it," said George.

Walter, I believe, came to the beach not only because he had known about the baby first, but because in some twisted way he felt as much responsible for its conception as George.

"If I hadn't gone off leaving Annie alone," Walter explained, "she and George never would have gotten back together."

"But you wanted her to go *with you*," George said.

"But I knew she never would," said Walter.

My father and Isabelle, too, were there for the baby.

Excited at the prospect of being first-time grandparents, they seemed newly in love with me, their entire family, and with each other. I caught them kissing out in the waves, and they would go off together for long walks down the beach. Sometimes I found Walter looking out at the two of them with a lost and wistful look. Was he thinking of his own summer with Isabelle? If so, he said nothing.

Even Yvette and Gregory seemed happy. Gregory told me silly jokes and Yvette read a book on child care that George had given her as a gift. We had already promised she could come to Connecticut to help me out when I first returned from the hospital, and she had smiled her prettiest of smiles at the news.

My father was now sticking his toes deep into the sand at the edge of the blanket; he buried them until they could no longer be seen. Then, pleased with himself, he gave me a kiss.

"Pregnant or skinny," he said loudly, "Annie is still the prettiest girl around."

"You bet," Walter said.

"What about me?" Isabelle said.

"You're not a girl," Yvette reminded her mother. "You're a woman."

"The prettiest woman," my father said, and that seemed to satisfy us all.

That afternoon after we had eaten lunch, Walter built the most elaborate sand castle I had ever seen. His accident had given him the patience he had never before possessed, and I was amazed at how he could sit and work with such concentration. There were turrets on the castle and a large moat, and tunnels traveling through its interior like a labyrinth. There was a drawbridge and bars on the two lowest windows. The children on the beach gathered around to watch him work, and when he ordered them to bring back pails of water or seashells shaped in a certain way, they swiftly obeyed.

The rest of us were also entranced. George had returned from his nap and he pronounced the castle the finest example of sand architecture he had ever seen. My father ran up to the house to find a flag for the castle's top. And Gregory and Yvette lorded it over the other children, that this artist, no matter how crippled, was *their* brother.

"Someday, I'm going to live in a castle just like that," Gregory said to the other children. Most of them were older then he and they giggled in disbelief.

"If you lived in a castle like that," Walter said. "Everything you ate would taste of sand."

"No, really," Gregory said.

Later of course the sea lapped at the castle's boundaries and we moved our blanket and umbrella further up the beach, where we could watch the destruction without getting wet ourselves. It seemed to take a long while, and then one large wave came up high and downed the entire castle, leaving only small wet mounds, mere traces of the grandeur that had been.

"It's so sad," Yvette said. "You worked so hard."

Walter shrugged. "It's the doing that counts."

"What does that mean?" Yvette said, but no one answered her.

We began to talk instead of other matters, such as who had the best tan, and what we would eat for dinner that night. Gregory wanted hamburgers on the grill, my father suggested we all go out. The ocean moved in closer and closer with the tide and no one moved. We were not tired, only lazy, and each time one of us thought of going back to the house to shower, to start dinner, the hot sun or just inertia made us change our mind.

"I'd like to stay here forever," my father said at one point. "Build an enclave for the family right here on the beach."

"I don't know," said Walter. "I would miss my exciting life in the city." He laughed a strange laugh, but he was the only one. For, of course, his life inside my father's apartment these last few months had been difficult and quiet, the rehabilitation slow. We all hoped he might move out on his own soon, or at least go back to work at the radio station, but Walter had made no mention of doing either. He did take walks by himself now, but when he returned he was winded and sad.

"Tomorrow I'm going to build a sand castle just like Walter's," Gregory said. "And it will be huge."

"Oh sure," Yvette said.

Finally, Isabelle stood up, shook the sand off her legs and arms, and began gathering up our belongings—towels, shirts, sandals, the lunch basket.

"I'm going in to cook dinner," she announced. "And you will all eat whatever I put on the table."

Gregory moaned. "I want hamburgers," he said, but he followed his mother back up the beach, his short legs taking three steps to her one. Soon after, Yvette and my father retrieved Walter's cane from the sand and helped him, one on each side, take his slow steps up toward the house. They stopped at one point, Walter waved to me, and then they continued on.

Only George and I were left, and as inevitably happened whenever we were alone this late in my pregnancy, our talk turned to the baby.

"Are you feeling okay?" George asked. I had been sick for most of the seven months with tiredness and nausea, and George had been attentive to my needs.

"I'm fine," I said.

"Is the baby still moving a lot?" he said.

"All the time," I said.

"Let's take a walk," George said, and I agreed. Barefoot, we walked down to where the water reached up to the sand, and we began to think of names. Although the due date was fast approaching, we did not yet have a name chosen. My father had told us he favored old-fashioned names like Maud and Horace.

"It will give the child character," he told us.

"It will give the child anguish," Walter had said. "Give the child a common name like John or Elizabeth. A name with no expectations."

Yvette and Gregory preferred the names of their friends at school, names like Jessica and Jennifer, Evan and Blaine.

"I always named my children after relatives," Isabelle had told us, but this too did not seem appropriate for George and me. Instead we thought of old friends, and characters in novels, and poured over name books, still never quite agreeing on what the other one suggested.

This evening was no different, and as the sun sank behind us we walked the beach calling names to each other out loud as if they were signals in some strange game.

"Alga," George suggested at one point.

"Coral," I said in reply.

"Starfish," said George. "Or how about Octopus?"

"Octopus?" I said, and though for a second I wondered if he was serious, I said nothing.

George was still easily bruised. His time in the hospital, our separation, were still issues we could not discuss or forget. He was quick to anger. So when I disagreed with his choices, I was tactful. "Not quite right," I would say, or "That one is good, but let's keep at it."

For a moment now, I thought he might offer, "Shark"

or "Dolphin," but instead he touched my belly with the tips of his fingers as if it were a kiss. "Okay," said George. "I'll keep trying."

And we both did, until we tired of the game and quit. We looked at the ocean, at each other, and did not imagine we were at all alike or that our lives would ever be what we hoped for when we were happiest and feeling most in love. Nevertheless, we held hands on the beach and I was sure any stranger passing by would grow misty-eyed at the scene—a pregnant woman, her husband, close and looking toward the future.

"We should really get back for dinner," I finally said. "I'm sure they're all waiting for us."

"Let's skip dinner," George said.

"I think I should eat," I said. But I knew we would miss dinner anyway. Neither would again be the first to leave.

As the sun set, the ocean was particularly calm, the air was smooth and still hot. I leaned against George and when my legs cramped, as they often did during my pregnancy, I struggled unsuccessfully to get into a comfortable position on the sand. I felt my large stomach like a metal weight, strapped on and locked in place.

"I hate this," I said to no one in particular. "I hate being pregnant."

George put his finger over my lips. "Don't say that, Anne," he warned. "It brings bad luck."

"Bad luck?" I said.

"For the baby," George said.

I felt our unnamed child shift its body and push slightly forward. Then, as if in protest at its confinement, it gave me a kick so hard, so intense, inside its sac, I lost my breath.

"Don't worry," I said to George when I recovered.

"We are only the parents, and it will be born just the same."

Then we did not talk about the baby anymore that night, and in the morning we forgot what was said and what was wrong as we tended to the many small tasks that bear upon our lives.